THREE BELLS, TWO BOWS AND ONE BROTHER'S BEST FRIEND

WILLA NASH

THREE BELLS, TWO BOWS AND ONE BROTHER'S BEST FRIEND

Editing & Proofreading:

Marion Archer, Making Manuscripts

www.makingmanuscripts.com

Karen Lawson, The Proof is in the Reading

Judy Zweifel, Judy's Proofreading

www.judysproofreading.com

Julie Deaton, Deaton Author Services

www.facebook.com/jdproofs

Cover:

Sarah Hansen © Okay Creations

www.okaycreations.com

OTHER TITLES

Calamity Montana Series

The Bribe

The Bluff

The Brazen

The Bully

Holiday Brothers Series

The Naughty, The Nice and The Nanny

Three Bells, Two Bows and One Brother's Best Friend

A Partridge and a Pregnancy

———

Writing as Devney Perry

Jamison Valley Series

The Coppersmith Farmhouse

The Clover Chapel

The Lucky Heart

The Outpost

The Bitterroot Inn

The Candle Palace

Maysen Jar Series

The Birthday List

Letters to Molly

Lark Cove Series

Tattered

Timid

Tragic

Tinsel

Clifton Forge Series

Steel King

Riven Knight

Stone Princess

Noble Prince

Fallen Jester

Tin Queen

CHAPTER ONE

STELLA

Jitters danced through my fingertips as I smoothed the fabric of my sweater. "How do I look?"

"Cute." My best friend, Wendy, inspected me head to toe. "But you can't wear those pants."

"Why not?" I spun sideways, checking out my butt in the mirror.

Wendy stood from my bed and handed me the green smoothie she'd brought over. "Drink this."

I took a sip from the straw and grimaced. "Blech. How can you stand this every day?"

"It's good for you. There's kale in it. Drink up," she ordered, disappearing into my walk-in closet.

"Eww." I took the smoothie to the trash can in the kitchen and tossed it in. It landed beside the smoothie she'd brought yesterday. Then I grabbed a red licorice stick from the open bag on the counter.

"Are you eating candy?" Wendy's eyes bugged out as she came out of my bedroom, a pair of distressed skinny jeans in her hand.

"Yes. I had an egg white omelet this morning for my health." I waved the licorice in the air. "This is for my happiness."

She frowned and thrust the jeans in my face. "Wear these."

"I'm not wearing jeans on my first day. My trousers are fine."

"They're too baggy."

"They're wide leg."

"They don't showcase your ass."

I rolled my eyes. "I'm trying to showcase my brain. Not my ass."

"But Heath is going to be there."

Heath. Just his name made my heart flutter. "It doesn't matter."

"Sure," she deadpanned.

"It doesn't. Not anymore. He's about to be my coworker and nothing more." That sounded so convincing I almost believed it myself. "I'm over it. I'm ready to meet a guy who actually notices me."

"Really?" Wendy asked.

"Yes. It was just a silly crush." A silly, fifteen-year-long crush.

Ever since my twelfth birthday when I'd stopped

believing that boys had cooties, I'd had a crush on Heath Holiday. My brother's best friend.

Of all my childhood fantasies, winning Heath was the only one that had lasted into my twenties—I'd given up hope of winning a Grammy because I was tone deaf and winning an Olympic medal because I had no athletic talent.

My crush on Heath had experienced its peaks and valleys. The occasional boyfriend would steal Heath's thunder from time to time. But the crush had endured.

Until now.

Two weeks ago, his father, Keith, had hired me as a project manager for his construction company. Heath and I were about to be coworkers at Holiday Homes, and it was time to smother my crush for good.

Fifteen years was long enough.

Once upon a time, I'd have worn tight pants in the desperate hope that he'd appreciate my ass and maybe, just maybe, see me as more than Guy's little sister. Those days were over.

"So does this mean you'll go out with Jake?" Wendy asked.

"No."

"Come on. He's so hot."

"Then you date him."

"We work together," she said. "That would be weird."

Jake, like Wendy, was a personal trainer at the biggest

gym in town. He was hot, she wasn't wrong. Except Jake knew exactly how hot he was and I had no desire to date a man who spent more than three hours a day staring in the mirror.

I finished my piece of licorice, and despite the scowl on her face, grabbed another.

"Okay, I'd better head to the gym. I've got a client at eight." She walked to the couch and swiped up her parka, pulling it on. "Good luck on your first day. I expect a full report."

"Aye, aye, Sheriff."

"That's not even close." She giggled. "Captain. Aye, aye, Captain."

"I'd much rather be a sheriff than a captain. I get seasick."

She laughed again and came over to give me a hug. "Consider pants that actually flatter your figure."

"I won't." I walked her to the front door, waving goodbye as she hurried through the crowded parking lot in my apartment complex. Then I rushed to my bathroom for one last check of my makeup and hair.

My blond locks were pulled away from my face in a tasteful—boring, professional—bun. My lips were stained a light pink, a classic but cute shade. My gray sweater was soft and fuzzy. Though I preferred bright, bold colors, today I was the epitome of plain. The only thing wild about my outfit was its appropriateness. Trousers and all.

Okay, maybe Wendy had a point. The pants were just a tiny bit . . . slouchy.

I stood in front of the mirror, turning sideways to glance over my shoulder at my butt. It looked . . . huge.

"This is why I don't wear these pants." I worried my bottom lip between my teeth, wiggling my rear in the mirror. No matter the angle, it looked twice its actual width and flat as a pancake.

So what? My coworkers wouldn't be looking at my ass. Impressing Heath wasn't the goal here, not that he'd notice.

A year ago, my brother had arranged a ski-slash-party weekend at Big Sky. Heath and I had both been there, and I'd paraded around that condo in my skimpiest bikini before taking a dip in the hot tub. Had he noticed me practically naked? *No.* A pair of tighter pants wouldn't make a difference.

Besides, I didn't care if he noticed me at work today, right? *Right.*

The reason I undid the clasp on the waistband and shoved the pants to the floor was not for Heath. It was for me. Because on your first day of work, you should love your outfit. That's why I was changing. Not for Heath. Not at all. Not even a little bit.

Kicking off my shoes, I raced through the house to the laundry room. My favorite black pants were in the dryer so I rifled through the heap, finding the right ones. I shoved my legs in, zipping them up as I hustled for the bedroom. With my heels on, I did one last check in the mirror. In these pants, I had an ass. A great ass.

"Much better."

Coat in hand, I headed outside. Snow blanketed the parking lot and streets around Bozeman, Montana. The shining sun made the drive across town to Holiday Homes blinding white.

My hometown was decked out for the holidays and had been since Thanksgiving. Evergreens were strung with colored lights. The old-fashioned lampposts along Main were adorned with garlands and bows. Window displays were teeming with fake snowdrifts and candy canes. This was my favorite time of year, the perfect day to start a new adventure.

Bozeman had changed during my twenty-seven years. The once sprawling farm fields on the outskirts of town were now filled with homes and businesses. Most of the faces at the grocery store were unfamiliar, though the smiles remained. Our small-town roots grew deep. I liked to believe that Bozeman's friendly culture was partly because of the families who'd lived here for generations, like my own. And the Holidays.

It was exciting to see the community grow and to be a part of this boom. Since graduating from college with a degree in business, I'd worked for a local construction company as a project manager. The homes they built were nice, albeit predictable. Spec houses and cookie-cutter blocks weren't overly appealing, so when I'd heard that Holiday Homes, the valley's premier custom home builder, was looking for someone to join their team, I'd tossed my name into the hat.

I had years of relevant experience and was damn good at my job. But if the reason they'd picked me out of all the other candidates was because Guy and Heath were best friends, well . . . this was my chance to prove myself.

Starting today.

My stomach did a somersault as I eased my SUV into the Holiday Homes parking lot. My hands shook as I parked and shut off the engine. But I couldn't seem to force myself out. I sat there and stared at the beautiful wood-sided building with enormous windows that gleamed beneath the blue sky.

The pay was nearly double what I'd been earning. With this salary, I might actually be able to afford a home in the next year so I could stop renting my apartment.

"Here we go." I sucked in a deep breath, then straightened my shoulders, grabbed my handbag and walked inside.

It smelled like coffee and sawdust, exactly as it had the day of my interview.

"Good morning," the receptionist greeted. Her long, gray hair was streaked with white. "Nice to see you again, Stella."

"Hi." My voice shook. "Nice to see you too."

"Excited for your first day?"

"And a little nervous."

"I've seen your résumé. You'll do great. I was actually

just going through your new employee paperwork." She stood and rounded the corner of her desk in the lobby, holding out a hand. "Gretchen."

"Of course. I remember you from the interview." I shook her hand, excitement radiating through my fingers.

Gretchen seemed like a no-nonsense person because we skipped the get-to-know-you small talk and she led me straight to my office. She spent twenty minutes getting me oriented with a phone, laptop and company email. Then she handed me a pile of paperwork that needed my signatures.

"Let's do an office tour," she said. "Then I'll let you go through this paperwork. Keith is at a customer meeting this morning but he should be in the office by ten."

"Sounds good." I nodded too wildly. My voice was still rattling with nerves. And damn it, when were my hands going to stop trembling?

"Keith's a great boss. I've worked here for fifteen years. You won't find a better family."

I opened my mouth to tell her I'd known the Holidays nearly my entire life, but clamped it shut and gave her another overly enthusiastic nod.

Maybe Gretchen knew that the Holidays had known me since my pigtail days. That I'd spent my childhood chasing Heath and his twin brother, Tobias, around the playground. Maybe she knew that I'd gone to their high school and college, and that our personal connection was likely the reason I was sitting at this desk.

But I didn't need to announce it to anyone. I was here to show this company, this team, that I was an asset. There was a chance favoritism had gotten me through the door. But I'd show every employee I could do this job.

Gretchen's office tour was a whirlwind of names and titles. Holiday Homes had grown from its start in Keith's garage thirty years ago to a twenty-person office staff and triple that on the labor crew.

The office building was two floors, the upstairs having most of the offices, including mine. On the first floor, there were three conference rooms with large, wood-paned windows. Next to them was a break room with a stainless-steel refrigerator, an espresso machine and two coffee pots.

Keith's corner office was dark and empty. The room beside it was also empty, though the lights were on. I didn't have to ask whose office it was. I caught a whiff of Heath's woodsy cologne.

I didn't let myself hold in that incredible smell. Not today. Because as of now, Heath was my coworker. My boss-type figure. A friend of my family. Nothing more.

"Heath must have snuck in while we were upstairs," Gretchen said. "I'm sure we'll find him."

I'd spent most of my life finding Heath. "Okay."

"He takes the lead on our larger builds, and the construction staff all report to him. You'll get to know the foremen and the crews with each project. They mostly come and go from the shop. We hold an all-staff meeting there once a month. And you'll see the guys on project sites."

"Can't wait to see it." Again.

The shop was on the other side of town, located in an industrial area of Bozeman and not far from a prominent lumber yard. It was completely out of my way from anything, work or home, but in high school, when I'd been at Bozeman High and Heath had been attending college at Montana State, I'd drive by the shop almost daily just in the hopes that I'd catch a glimpse of him.

During summer breaks from college, he'd be the guy at the shop reloading trailers with supplies. I'd spot him occasionally, sweating and gorgeous, loading boards onto a flatbed truck.

"Tobias?" Gretchen poked her head into the next office over.

"Come on in, Gretchen." A familiar face greeted me with a wide, white smile. Tobias stood from his desk and rounded the corner to sit on its edge. "Hey, Stella. Welcome aboard."

"Thanks." I smiled at Tobias, my nerves taking on a whole new edge.

Yep, this is weird.

This was Tobias, my childhood friend. The kid who'd chased Guy and me around my living room when we'd played tag. The boy who had once accidentally walked in on me in the bathroom while I was peeing.

Now he was basically my superior. As the architect at

Holiday Homes, he'd be giving me orders and making sure I followed through.

If he felt any of the same awkwardness, he didn't let it show. "How's it going so far?"

"Great. Gretchen has been showing me around. I'm sure she'll be sick of answering my questions before the day is over."

"Pfft." She waved it off. "I'm here to help. Whatever you need."

"Gretchen, you remember our friend Guy Marten, right?" Tobias asked her. "Stella is his sister."

"Oh, I hadn't put that together," Gretchen said. "But now that you mention it, I can see the resemblance."

Guy and I both had blond hair, though his was a shade darker than mine. We had the same hazel eyes and narrow noses. But where he was always goofing off, content only if he was earning laughs and standing in the center of attention, I'd been the girl who loved the quiet moments most. The girl who swam or hiked or lost herself in a book. My Friday nights were typically spent in flannel pajamas with a bowl of popcorn and the latest hit show.

"Since you know Heath, I guess we don't need to track him down," Gretchen said, then checked her watch. "Okay, we've got a little time before Keith gets in. I'll let you chat and then settle into your office. Would you like some coffee?"

"I can find it. Thanks, Gretchen."

"Like Tobias said, welcome aboard. We're a family

here at Holiday and are so excited to have you here. Keith was so impressed by your interview. He's probably going to dump a bunch of stuff on you today."

"She can handle it." A deep, rugged voice came from the doorway.

I glanced over and my stupid heart tumbled.

Heath leaned against the threshold, his hands tucked into his jeans pockets. "Hey, Stell."

"Hey, Heath." *Don't blush. Don't blush. Please, don't blush.*

My cheeks felt hot, despite my silent commands. I'd been fighting that damn blush for what felt like my whole life.

Why couldn't I see Heath the way I saw Tobias? A friend, nothing more. They had the same dark hair. The same piercing blue eyes. The same soft lips and straight nose. Hell, Tobias had even grown a beard and I'd always thought beards were sexy.

But did my face flame for *that* Holiday brother? No. Never. Not once.

There was something different about Heath.

Maybe it was how whenever he wore a button-down shirt, he'd roll the sleeves up his sculpted forearms. Maybe it was the way his smile was a little crooked on the right side. Maybe it was the way he laughed often and believed cookies were a major food group.

Heath was . . . Heath. A cute boy who'd grown into a ridiculously handsome man. He was the dream.

The dream I needed to banish. Effective immediately.

He pushed off the door's frame to stride into Tobias's office, standing close, but not too close. His cologne wrapped around me like a warm hug. His six-foot-two frame dwarfed my five-four, and I had to tilt up my chin as his blue eyes drew me in. "How's the first day going?"

"Good." My voice was breathy. Though considering it was always breathy when he was in the same room, he probably thought it was normal. Gretchen and Tobias would not. I cleared my throat, dropping it a bit. "How are you?"

Too low. Damn it. Now I sounded like I was impersonating a man.

Gretchen was staring.

I simply smiled. *Nothing strange here, Gretch. Everything is normal. Totally normal.*

"Busy," Heath answered. Right, I'd asked a question. "Thursdays are always hectic."

Thursday was a strange day to start a new job, but when I'd given my former employer my two weeks' notice, he'd asked for a few more days to wrap up the project I'd been working on.

"Did you get an office?" he asked.

"Yep. Gretchen got me all settled."

"Good deal." He nudged my elbow with his. And there went my cheeks again. *Shit.* "I'm getting some coffee. I'll come up and visit later. Guy told me something about a clogged toilet. You'll have to tell me how that all turned out."

My mouth fell open.

Why, of all the things that Guy and Heath could discuss, was the fact that I'd clogged my toilet something conversation-worthy?

I hated my brother. I actually *hated* my brother.

Guy wouldn't even have known about the toilet incident had he not come over while I'd been mopping the bathroom floor with towels.

"It was nothing." I looked to Tobias and Gretchen, my new coworkers who didn't need to think I had plumbing issues—with my house or my bowels. "I was cleaning and the top of my toilet wand, the disposable ones, didn't go down like it should have. My dad came over and snaked it clear for me. All fixed now. And from now on I'll only be flushing the number ones and twos."

Oh. My. God.

Why, Stella? Why?

The room was silent for a beat, then Gretchen smiled and excused herself. Tobias chuckled and went back to his chair. And I slid past Heath, slinking away for the break room.

I swallowed a groan. So it wasn't the best way to start this off. Not the worst, but not the best. But considering my history of embarrassing moments with Heath, I'd settle for a strange toilet discussion.

It was better than the time I'd gotten my period at the

park when I was fourteen. Heath and Guy had been out tossing a football and I'd decided to go out there with a book and a blanket, hoping Heath would talk to me. I'd had on my cutest pair of white shorts.

Guy had spotted—literally—it first. He'd declared, right in front of Heath, that I needed to go home and get a tampon.

It was arguably the worst of my embarrassing moments.

Though a close second runner-up was the time in seventh grade when Heath had been over to play video games with Guy. I'd stopped by the living room to watch. Mom had made eggs that morning and eggs always made my stomach rumble. I'd been sitting there, hanging on Heath's every word. He'd said something funny. I'd laughed. And farted. The noise and smell had chased them from the room.

Clogged toilet? No sweat. I'd survived much, much worse. The rest of my day would be nothing but normal. I'd get some coffee, then breeze through the paperwork in my new office before my meeting with Keith.

"Mugs . . ." I opened the cupboards above the coffee pots in the break room, finding them all empty. "Okay, maybe I don't need coffee."

"Mugs are over here." Heath strode in, going for the cabinet beside the fridge. "I told Dad that this was not the logical place to keep them but he likes them beside the dishwasher."

"Ah. Well, for the record, I agree with you."

"Thanks." He grinned and handed me a white, ceramic mug. "Glad you're here. We've been swamped and it will be great to have someone with experience."

"I'm excited to be here too." I filled my mug and smiled. "I liked my other job, but I think this will fit my interests more. I really do love the homes you guys build."

Holiday Homes was known for its meticulous attention to detail. For the past five years, each of their showcases in the annual Parade of Homes had been my favorite.

"We've got some fun projects coming up too," Heath said.

"Good." I raised my mug in a salute. "I'd better get going on my new employee paperwork. See you later."

He nodded. "Have a good day."

I walked away, entirely impressed with myself that I'd made it through that exchange without flushed cheeks or rambling nonsense.

Obviously, I'd spoken to Heath many, many times. But usually, Guy was there to tease me or goof around. Now that we were working together, maybe Heath would see me as an adult if we spent some time away from my brother.

I was a step away from the door when Heath called my name.

"Stella."

"Yeah?" I turned.

He walked over, coming straight into my space.

My breath hitched as he stopped so close that the heat from his chest radiated against my body.

He bent, his large, strong body dropping to a crouch. His fingers brushed my calf.

I watched stunned, speechless, as he stood tall and held out a small scrap of black lace.

A thong.

My thong.

My thong that had been stuck to my pants all. Freaking. Morning. During my time with Gretchen. During the tour to meet my new coworkers. During my break room conversation with Heath.

There wasn't a word for this level of mortification.

"Um . . ." He held out my thong.

I swiped it from his hand, utterly stunned. If I hadn't changed my pants, if I'd just worn the trousers, static cling wouldn't have been an issue. Yet here I was, wearing tight pants with a pair of panties in my fist.

The period and fart incidents paled in comparison.

Heath gave me a small smile, then slipped past me and strode down the hallway to his office.

"Oh. My. God." I set my coffee aside and buried my flaming-red face in my hands.

When it came to Heath Holiday, I was doomed.

CHAPTER TWO

HEATH

"Any chance you could get me the Winthrop bid by tomorrow?" Dad asked.

"Ha." I chuckled. "No."

He frowned. "Why not?"

"Because it's third on my list." I tapped my pen on the notepad in front of me. "You told me that the Grant and Freeman bids were priority."

"Damn," he muttered. "We have too many priorities."

"You're not joking."

"Hopefully if Stella gets up to speed quickly, we can shift some of these projects from your plate to hers."

"That would be great." At this point, I couldn't keep up with the estimates let alone tracking every build, because I was being pulled in seven different directions.

Even in December, a month when business should have been slower than average, our crews were struggling

to keep up with demand. It was too cold to pour founda-
tions for new builds, but we had enough homes in progress
that every construction team was assigned to a jobsite.
Most were putting in overtime on framing or flooring or
one of many other tasks that didn't start with the letter f
but my brain was so fried I'd forgotten them at the
moment.

"I'm late for dinner and your mom's going to be mad.
I'd better head home." Dad stood from his chair across
from my desk. "See you tomorrow."

"Yep. Bye, Dad."

He waved and walked out, swinging by his corner
office to grab his laptop and coat before the lights flickered
off.

"Bye, Dad," Tobias said from his office. Five minutes
later, after the shuffle of paperwork and closing of desk
drawers, he hollered down the hallway, "I'm leaving
too."

"See ya," I called back.

"Want me to lock up?"

"I'll do it."

"Don't stay too late." His footsteps echoed on the
hickory floors as he made his way through the lobby and
out the front door.

If there was any chance of me taking off the week
between Christmas and New Year's, I'd definitely be
staying late.

The quiet settled in the building, and I sank deeper

into my chair, facing the mountain of work on my desk. It was daunting. Good thing I didn't mind a challenge.

Dad wanted the Winthrop job estimated so I reached for the Winthrop file. I fished out the notes I'd made during our last meeting and found the rough sketch that Tobias had put together after his initial consult.

He was our only architect at the moment. His predecessor had retired this spring and Tobias had stepped in to fill his shoes. My brother was just as busy as I was after New Year's. We'd talked about finding another architect to join the team.

While Tobias loved the planning, the measurements and the tiny details, I simply liked to get shit done. I liked to watch a bare patch of dirt be transformed into a home. As long as the construction was quality and our clients were happy, I didn't care if the roof style was gable, hip or mansard.

For Dad's succession plan, our varied interests had worked out perfectly. He didn't have to choose a son to take over management because Tobias had no interest in replacing him as the general manager. That position would fall to me while my brother would happily spend his days at a drafting desk.

Dad was nowhere near ready to retire, and at twenty-nine, I was nowhere near ready to take over. I had too much to learn from Dad. I had too much respect for him to step on his shoes.

So for now, I managed the foremen and their staff

while putting together estimates for our largest and most pretentious jobs. Dad supervised the project managers who acted as the liaisons with the foremen to make sure the customers were happy and that schedules and budgets were on track. In the past year, we'd hired three new project managers, and still, we couldn't keep up.

Holiday Homes was growing. And with it, so were my hours.

I pushed away from my desk, hitting the break room for a glass of water. Then I came back to my office and got to work. I was about halfway through my notes on the Winthrop project when a noise echoed from the ceiling. My fingers froze above the keyboard. "What the hell?"

Another noise had me standing and hustling to the stairs. Everyone should have gone home already. The lights in the hallway were off. Every office was dark.

Except one.

Stella's.

What was she still doing here? It was her first day. If anyone should have headed home by now, it was her.

Stella's feet were bare, her heels discarded by the window. The sleeves of her sweater were bunched at her elbows as she scrambled to pick up ice cubes off the floor.

"What are you doing?"

"Ah!" she screamed, her face whipping to the door. "Oh my God, you scared me."

"Sorry." I held up my hands, stepping into the office. "I thought I was the only one left, then I heard a noise."

"I bumped my glass over. It was empty except for the ice." She plucked up three more cubes, dropping them into the glass before standing to her feet.

Her hair was coming out of its knot, a few long, blond tendrils framing her face.

Stella Marten was one of the most beautiful women I'd ever seen.

And my best friend's sister.

I don't get to think she's beautiful. I'd been reminding myself that for years.

I didn't get to drown in those hazel eyes or think about kissing her soft lips. I didn't get to fantasize about her toned legs wrapped around my hips or the fact that I'd had her panties in my hand this morning.

Off-limits. Stella had always been off-limits.

"How was your first day?" I asked, walking into the room and taking the single empty chair opposite hers at the desk.

"Good." She sank into her chair, swiveling it back and forth. There was more paperwork on the desk than I'd expected to see. "Your dad believes in drinking from a fire hose, doesn't he?"

"Two fire hoses." I laughed. "What did he give you?"

"The Jensen remodel."

I cringed.

"That bad?"

"It's over budget and behind schedule."

I expected a groan. Maybe a string of expletives. But Stella sat straighter and nodded. "I'll fix it."

"I believe you can."

Stella, like me, didn't back down from many challenges. Even though she was two years younger, as kids, she'd always kept up with Guy, Tobias and me. On our bikes, no matter how hard she'd had to pedal, she'd kept pace. At the swimming pool, when we'd dared her to try the high dive, she'd plugged her nose and jumped. And at the ski hill, when we'd all attempted our first black diamond, she'd followed us down the mountain.

"Thanks." Her cheeks colored.

That blush of hers was as pretty as her eyes. I'd seen it countless times in my life and it never got old.

"So what can you tell me about the Jensen project?" she asked.

"Well . . . it's been a disaster from the start, partly because we didn't have the time to take it on and should have turned it down. But Dad is friends with Joe Jensen and didn't want to say no. Then, because we didn't turn it down and no one had time, it hasn't really had a primary resource. We've all chipped in, here and there, but what it needs is a driver to see it through."

"I can do that." She nodded at the mess of papers on her desk. "As soon as I make sense of this."

"I did the original estimate. I think they've had a few change orders since, but I can go through the details with you if you'd like."

"Really? That would be great."

"How about now?"

"If you don't mind."

"Not at all." I had other work to do, but in the past year, I'd found it harder and harder to stay away from Stella.

I blamed it on that damn party Guy had organized last year at Big Sky. Stella had come along to ski, then party at the condo. She'd taken a dip in the hot tub every night and the image of her in that orange bikini was burned into my brain.

It was like a lightbulb had turned on. Stella wasn't Stella, my friend's little sister and the tagalong. Stella was *Stella*.

Beautiful. Smart. Charming. Sexy.

I liked Stella.

Despite the reasons I shouldn't.

I carried my chair around to her side of the desk as she slid over a file folder. Then we dove in, spending the next hour going through the drawings, schedule and progress update notes.

"Tomorrow, let's find an hour, and I'll take you out to the jobsite."

"Thanks, Heath."

"You're welcome."

Her eyes met mine, and for a moment, I almost leaned in. For a year, I'd been tempted to cross the line. To taste the lips I'd wanted to taste for months. But Guy's voice rang in my head.

Off-limits.

"This project seems to be costing a hand and a foot, doesn't it?" she asked.

"Huh?" I blinked. "A hand and . . . oh. You mean it costs an arm and a leg. That's the saying."

"A hand and a foot seem less extreme than an arm and a leg." She waved it off. "You know how sayings go. Potato, tomato."

"Also not a saying."

"Po-tah-toe, toe-mah-toe."

I fought a smile. "Still not right."

"It makes sense to me." She shrugged. "Disagree to agree."

"That's . . ." I lost the battle and laughed. God, she was funny. In the way that she never tried to be funny.

She was just . . . Stella.

"It's late." I relaxed into my chair. "I was planning on ordering in some dinner. Want to stick around and eat? Or are you ready to get out of here?"

"I could eat."

"What do you feel like?"

"Whatever you want. Surprise me."

I pulled my phone from my pocket and opened the Door Dash app. I'd had enough meals at the Marten house to know that Stella loved pepperoni pizza. With it ordered, I nodded to the papers on her desk. "Besides the Jensen project, what else did my dad give you?"

"That's the only project for now, but he mentioned some general organization stuff. During my interview, I told him how I'd researched this new project management software for my old company. I put this entire pitch together about how it worked and how it could improve efficiency and customer communication, but my boss didn't want to show it to the owner. He said our processes worked fine, so why change them?"

"Ah. Is that why you left?"

"Partly. I also really like the homes you guys build."

"They're the best." Pride laced my voice.

Dad had established Holiday Homes with his two hands, blood, sweat and back-breaking hours. His standards had been passed down to our craftsmen, and he never settled for less than exceptional. He might not wield a hammer these days, but he hired men who shared his craftsmanship. They built homes that they'd all be proud to live in themselves.

"What's the software?" I asked.

"It's just a client interface. The customers can log in to see their schedules and invoices. It's where you'd process change orders. The crew takes pictures of their progress each day so we can upload the photos into a dashboard. It makes the entire process more transparent. Which is probably why my old boss didn't want to do it. It would be harder to hide missed dates."

"Dad's a big advocate for being upfront about the schedule. I bet he started salivating about this."

She smiled. "He was pretty excited."

"Dad's all about organization these days. He feels like we've got a solid crew, but we're short-staffed on the business side of things." Considering Stella and I were both here after dark, he wasn't wrong.

"What do you think?" she asked.

It was the first time anyone had asked me that question in a while. "I think sometimes Dad wants to make this business perfect so that when he retires, it's smooth sailing for me and Tobias. Except he forgets that neither of us mind some rough waters."

"You'd get bored if it was perfect."

"Yeah, I would." A familiar feeling settled in my chest. A feeling I usually got around Stella. Talking to her was like talking to my oldest friend. She knew me, understood me, arguably better than anyone else, including her brother.

Stella was more insightful. Maybe it was just a female thing, but she asked the questions guys didn't often ask.

My comfort with her was just another reason that she'd been tempting me for a year. The bikini incident had opened my eyes, but if I was being honest with myself, I'd been drawn to Stella for a lot longer. Which was why I tore my gaze away from her beautiful face and stood, returning the chair to the other side of the desk.

"I'm keeping you from your work," she said. "Sorry."

"Don't apologize. I'm going to head downstairs." I needed to put a staircase between us before I did something dumb. "I'll holler when dinner gets here."

"Okay. Thanks again."

"Always." I smiled and disappeared.

My office was cold compared to hers and didn't smell half as good without her sweet perfume, but small interactions with Stella were necessary. Otherwise, my body would get ideas about doing things to hers. Dirty, delicious things.

The delivery guy was prompt, and before I'd resecured the boundaries with Stella, he came into the building. I traded him a seven-dollar tip for a pepperoni pizza, then set it up in the break room before taking the stairs two at a time.

Stella was focused on the Jensen file when I reached her office, a pen in her hand and a pencil between her lips.

To be that pencil.

I swallowed hard. "Dinner's here."

Her eyes flew to the door and her mouth fell open, the pencil dropping. "Be right there."

Damn, but she was pretty with her hair falling out and her guard down.

I forced myself away, dragging a hand over my face. What the hell was wrong with me tonight? As of today, we were coworkers. Another reason to keep our relationship strictly platonic.

When Dad had hired her, I'd told him it was a great

decision. Stella would be an asset to our team. Except maybe shoving my attraction aside might be harder than I'd realized. We'd be spending time together. I'd see her daily.

Off-limits.

Whatever was going on with me, I needed to get my shit together and fast because Stella wasn't going anywhere. We worked together now, and Guy would cut off my balls if I dared touch his sister.

What would he say if he knew I'd had her panties in my hand today?

Poor Stella. I chuckled to myself as I took out plates and forks and napkins in the break room. I doubted anyone else had seen her thong. Gretchen would have told her if she'd noticed. The only reason I'd spotted it was because I'd been checking Stella out, drinking in those long legs and those perfectly fitted black pants. Not too loose. Not too tight. Just sexy as fuck.

The thong had been clinging to her hemline, almost dropping to her heels. The image of her wearing only those stilettos and that thong popped into my head and my cock jerked behind the zipper of my jeans.

Don't think about Stella naked. Don't think about Stella naked.

"Fuck my life," I muttered.

"What?"

I turned to see Stella behind me. "Oh, nothing. Just thinking about a job."

A blow job.

Goddamn it, Holiday. I gestured to the table, taking the chair in the corner.

Stella sat opposite me and flipped open the pizza box, closing her eyes as she dragged in the scent of garlic and cheese. "I love pepperoni pizza."

"I know."

She opened her eyes and took a slice, moaning at the first bite. "I was starving."

I watched her chew, the way her lips moved and the satisfaction on her face as she closed her eyes again, her entire focus on tasting her food. That was how Stella did most things. With intent. She'd always had this way of savoring the tastes, smells and sounds that the rest of us took for granted.

In my world of endless distraction, Stella made me stop and take pause.

A drop of sauce leaked off the slice and landed on her sweater, right at the upper swell of her left breast.

I stared, my mouth watering to lick it away.

"Seriously?" She set her pizza down and dove for the napkins. "I swear you are cursed."

"You're not curs—wait. Did you say *I'm* cursed?"

"Well, yeah." She blotted at the sauce but all it did was make the orange stain grow. Finally she gave up, balling the napkins and tossing them aside. "Damn it. This was a new sweater."

"I'm sure it will come out. But you didn't answer my question. Why am I cursed?"

"Because my most embarrassing moments all happen when you're around." She gestured to her sweater. "Example one. Example two is the thong in my purse."

I grinned. "So that makes me cursed."

"Absolutely. The list goes on and on. Remember that time Guy bought a Slip 'N Slide my sophomore year? You and Tobias came over to try it out and dared me to do it too. Which I did."

"And your top came off." The image of her bare breasts as she'd streaked into the house was crystal clear, even all these years later.

That pretty pink flush crept into her cheeks. "See? You're cursed. That was horrific."

"I didn't mind," I teased. "That Slip 'N Slide incident was one of my favorite memories from high school."

"Cursed." She reached for her pizza and took a bite.

I took my own piece, turning my attention to eating so I wouldn't think more about Stella's breasts. But that orange stain was like a beacon to her chest, and after my tenth glance, I knew it was time to call this day quits. Before I made a mistake.

"Want any more?" I asked, and when she shook her head, I flipped the lid on the box closed, taking it to the fridge. "Are you about done tonight?"

"Yeah. Thanks for dinner."

"You're welcome." I nodded to the door. "It's dark. Grab your stuff and I'll walk you out."

"Okay." She collected the trash and put it in the garbage can, then slipped out of the room.

"Hell." I rubbed a hand over my face.

This had to stop. For good.

I'd made a promise years ago and had kept it for too long to break it now.

Guy had always been protective of Stella, in his own way. He teased her mercilessly. But behind her back, he'd been a pit bull since high school, barking at any male who'd so much as glanced in her direction.

The day she'd walked into Bozeman High as a freshman, a shy, beautiful girl, Stella had turned a lot of heads. Guy had made me promise that if anyone made a move on his sister, I'd help kick their ass. He'd spread that word and no one had been stupid enough to cross him and ignite his infamous temper.

Guy was right to watch out for Stella. Sweet, sweet Stella.

I went to my office and grabbed my coat and keys, then walked to the lobby and waited for her. When the click of her heels sounded on the stairs, I looked up and my mouth went dry.

She'd taken her hair out. The blond strands draped around her face and hung down nearly to her waist. That hair had been a part of many adult fantasies.

"Ready?" she asked.

"Yeah. Let's get out of here." Fast. I strode to the door, holding it open for her. Then I locked up the office and fell into step beside her as we crossed the parking lot to her SUV.

"See you tomorrow, Heath."

"Bye, Stell." I walked to my truck, climbing in and waiting until she reversed out of her spot and pulled onto the street. Then I let out a frustrated groan.

She was off-limits.

Why did that make me want her even more?

Of all the women in the world, why was Stella the one who tempted me? Maybe she was right.

I was cursed.

CHAPTER THREE

STELLA

"This is fantastic," Keith said.

I beamed under his praise. "Thank you."

"I vote we buy it." He rapped his knuckles on the conference room table. "Everyone good with this?"

Heath, Tobias and the other two project managers who'd watched my presentation all agreed.

"I'm excited to try out this software," Tobias said, glancing at his phone, then pushing his chair away from the table. "Great suggestion, Stella. I've got to duck out for a call."

"And I've got a date with my lovely wife so I'm taking off too," Keith said. "I'll be out most of next week. Maddox is coming home so I'll be sticking close to the house. But I'm a phone call away if you need anything."

Keith stood and made his way to the door with the project managers shuffling out close behind.

Leaving Heath and me alone.

I breathed for what felt like the first time in an hour.

"Good job, Stell."

"Did I do okay? Be honest."

"You did awesome." His smile was contagious.

I'd found Heath's gaze often as I'd given my pitch today. Not only because his blue eyes were the most alluring in any room, but because over the past two weeks, something had shifted between us.

The nerves that normally came with seeing him had subsided. Maybe because we saw each other every day, either in the break room or when we crossed paths in the hallways. Maybe I was getting over my crush—*probably not*. Whatever the reason, the swarm of yellowjackets in my stomach that usually accompanied Heath's smile had moved on and found a new hive.

Butterflies had taken up their place. Delicate and lovely butterflies that had fluttered each time he'd given me a sure nod while I'd demoed the software I'd told him about on my first day.

"I thought it would take longer." I glanced at the clock on the wall. "Is it bad that there weren't many questions?"

"Your presentation was solid." He leaned his elbows on the table. "I had questions but you answered them all."

"Okay, good." I shut the lid on my laptop. "Then I'm calling it a win."

"A big win." He shoved out of his chair. "We should celebrate. Want to head downtown for a drink?"

Ooh . . . bad idea. In the past two weeks I'd managed to avoid any other embarrassing moments with Heath, but it was only a matter of time before the curse returned. Adding alcohol to the mix would surely accelerate the inevitable.

Say no. "Sure."

"Grab your stuff. Meet you in the lobby in five." He strode out of the conference room, and I smacked a hand to my forehead.

Weak. So weak. But it was too late to take it back—that and I didn't want to take it back because this was Heath—so I scrambled to collect the materials from my presentation and head upstairs to my office where I put everything away. With my camel wool coat pulled on and a gray blanket scarf wrapped around my shoulders, I grabbed my purse and slung it over a shoulder.

Flipping the lights off in my office, I moved toward the staircase, hearing a familiar voice echo from the lobby.

"Guy, you'd better stop flirting with me," Gretchen warned. "I'm old enough to be your mother."

"You say that every time I come in here."

"And you never listen."

"Nope." My brother chuckled, and with his laugh, my spirits sank. So much for a celebratory drink with Heath. Guy would hijack the night and steal his best friend.

Damn.

The clomp of my heels as I trudged down the stairs

drew his attention and he smiled when he spotted me. "Hey, Stella Bells."

"Hi. What are you up to?"

"Thought I'd see if Heath wanted to head downtown. Grab a drink."

"Oh. Great," I lied.

"Hey." Heath came down the hallway from his office, shrugging on his black coat. Combined with his dark hair and rugged voice, that coat was sexier than it should have been. Oh, what I wouldn't do to shove it off those broad shoulders.

Yeah, my crush wasn't entirely dead.

"You up for a drink?" Guy asked him.

"Actually, we were just heading downtown. Celebrating Stella's successful presentation today."

"We don't need to." I waved it off. "You guys go without me."

"Come on, Stell." Heath nudged my elbow with his. "One drink."

"Or three," Guy teased. "For me. You can be my designated driver."

Being the third or fourth wheel hadn't bothered me as a kid. But now it felt . . . pathetic. And I had no desire to be Guy's chauffeur.

"Or . . ." Heath shot him a flat look. "You can call a cab."

"I'm just kidding." Guy shrugged. "Mostly I like it

when Stella drives because she's the safest drive in Gallatin County."

Yes, I typically drove five miles per hour below the speed limit, but I'd never had a ticket or gotten into an accident.

"Come with us, Stella," Guy pleaded. "Don't be boring."

"Fine," I muttered. I loved my brother. I adored Heath. But the two of them together weren't always easy to be around. Not because of Heath but because of Guy.

He had no filter and loved to tease. Most of the time he'd forget I wasn't one of the guys. The last time we'd gone out, a bunch of his college fraternity brothers had been in town for the homecoming football game. He'd coerced me into going out with them, and the group had traded stories for hours about the women they'd screwed.

As the drinks had flowed, the stories had become more and more far-fetched, and finally, after three hours, I'd told Guy he could find a different ride home. The only good thing about that night was that Heath hadn't been there. I don't think I would have been able to handle hearing him describe his sexual escapades with other women.

Though I doubted he would have shared anyway. Heath had never been that sort of man.

At least, not around me.

But Guy had a way of bringing out the crude, and whenever he and Heath were drinking together, I'd made it a point to stay away. One glass of wine and then I'd go home to trade my jeans for a pair of pajama pants.

We drove separately downtown. Parking was a nightmare because Main was a popular place for holiday work functions and parties, but I managed to find a spot two blocks away from the bar where we were meeting. I left my car in the snow-covered lot, then headed for the bar.

I'd just rounded the corner of the sidewalk when a rumbling voice called my name.

"Stella."

I glanced over my shoulder to see Heath rushing to catch up.

His long legs ate up the distance between us. Under the faint streetlamps, he looked unbelievably sexy. His jaw chiseled. His hair finger-combed off his forehead. His lips soft and supple.

I used the moments it took for him to reach my side to stop my heart from doing cartwheels. There would be no acrobatics. We were coworkers. Friends, maybe? Nothing more.

"Hey." Damn. My breathy voice was back after a two-week hiatus in the office. I hadn't missed it.

"Ready?"

"Is anyone really ready to go drinking with Guy?"

"True." He laughed. "You might think you're ready. But you never are."

I smiled and fell into step beside him, turning my face

to the decorations strung across the street. "I love that they still string the same garland that they did when I was little."

"Same here. Mom and Dad used to bring us down here for the Christmas Stroll each year. So much around Bozeman has changed, but I love that this is the same."

The green, gold and ruby garland draped over Main in thick, glittering strands. Wreaths had been hung on the doors of most businesses. Golden twinkle lights illuminated the trees, making them sparkle against the background of the black, winter sky.

The temperature was creeping toward zero, but downtown, it felt warmer with the scent of apple cinnamon and pine clinging to the air.

So busy glancing around, I missed a patch of ice on the sidewalk and my heel caught it, nearly sending me crashing to my knees. Except a strong arm wrapped around my waist, pinning me to an equally strong body.

"Whoa." Heath stopped, holding me up until my legs were steady.

"See? You're cursed. I haven't slipped on ice in years."

He chuckled, loosening his grip. "Yes. It was my fault that you weren't paying attention."

"Exactly."

"To be safe." He took my forearm and tucked it beside his ribs, holding my arm as he started down the sidewalk again.

I caught our reflection in a shop window and my

breath hitched. We looked like a couple. A hot couple. I bit my lip to hide a smile and kept walking. There was no harm in pretending for a block, right?

Our journey ended too soon, and when we reached the bar, Heath let go of my arm to open the door.

Guy was waiting at a table with three shots already lined up. Knowing my brother, they were all for himself.

"This is going to be interesting," I muttered.

"Your brother is nothing if not entertaining." Heath touched my elbow. "Think you can make it to the table on your own or do you suspect I'll twist your ankle?"

"Har har," I deadpanned, then joined my brother. After we took our coats off, he surprised me by sliding a shot to Heath and me.

"Cheers." He raised his glass, waiting just long enough for ours to clink his before he tossed the tequila back. "So Mel and I broke up today."

"Oh, Guy." I pressed a hand to my heart. "I'm sorry."

He shrugged. "No big deal."

Liar. It was a big deal. He and Mel had dated on and off in high school, but had broken up for the final time before heading to college. They'd kept in touch over the years, and when she'd moved back to Bozeman a few months ago, they'd started dating again.

Guy had talked about Mel all the time. He'd even told me that this time around, it might be the real deal.

"What happened?" Heath asked.

"She wanted to be done, so now we're done." He slid off his stool. "You guys want another shot? Because I do."

Without waiting for us to answer, he stalked toward the bar and flagged down the bartender. This time, his three shots were just for him. He threw them down his throat in quick succession, then clapped and forced a too-wide smile.

"Check her out." My brother jerked his chin over my shoulder.

I shifted, following his gaze to a brunette standing at the bar wearing a tight yellow dress and over-the-knee boots. Not exactly winter apparel but she did make a statement. A redhead in a similar dress, this one pink, joined her friend, the two of them scanning the bar.

Hunting. They were hunting.

And Guy would gladly become their prey.

Technically, I'd had my drink. Could I leave now?

I should have known this would happen when Guy had suggested the Rocking R Bar. It was his favorite bar and where I suspected he picked up most of his women. It was typically a college hangout, but this close to Christmas, most students were into finals and the bar was mostly people our age, adults in their twenties and thirties.

"That brunette's eye-fucking you, Holiday." Guy grinned. "Get over there."

Annnnnd it was time for me to go.

"Nah." Heath didn't so much as look toward the

women. "We're here to celebrate Stella's successful first two weeks at work."

"Don't be lame," Guy said.

Heath's jaw clenched. "Don't be an asshole."

"Whatever. So work's been good?" Guy asked me.

"Yeah, I like it."

"She's doing a hell of a job." Heath gave me a little smile.

"Of course she is." Guy clapped his hand on my shoulder. "You guys were lucky to steal her. Stella's a rock star."

"Thanks." Yes, Guy could be a huge, blunt idiot. But he also had so much confidence in me that it gave me confidence in myself. Whenever I was unsure, he'd tell me I could do anything I set my mind to.

"Welcome." My brother nodded, then glanced around the bar. "Hey, look. It's that guy you had a crush on, Stella."

"W-what?"

The only guy who I'd crushed on was Heath. But there was no way Guy would call me out here, now, would he? No way. Guy was a jerk sometimes but that would be cruel.

"Joel? Isn't that his name?" Guy pointed to the other side of the bar.

I spotted who he was talking about and my heart climbed out of my throat. "Yes, his name is Joel. But no, I never had a crush on him."

"Yes, you did."

"Pretty sure I didn't." Joel and I had gone to college together, and this crush Guy was thinking of had been the other way around. "He liked me. I wasn't interested."

"That's right. Because you were too busy drooling over Heath." Guy laughed, oblivious to what he'd just said.

Meanwhile, my heart splattered on the table. *Ouch.* Tonight, the humiliation was courtesy of my brother.

"Jesus, Guy," Heath clipped. "What the hell?"

My brother scoffed. "It's not like we all don't know she was into you for like a decade. Who cares?"

Heath's jaw clenched. "Shut up, Guy."

"What's wrong with you two tonight?" My brother scoffed. "I thought we were here to have some fun."

"I think I'm all *funned* out." I stood from my stool, grabbed my coat, scarf and purse, then headed for the door, not even bothering to bundle up for the cold.

Tears pricked at the corners of my eyes as I flew out the door. I huffed it down one block, pulling on my coat as I walked, and by the time I made it down the second, the sting in my nose and the burn in my throat made it hard to breathe.

Why would he say that? Now, of all times. Heath and I weren't just acquaintances anymore but coworkers. Why was my brother such a dickhead? Guy had always teased me, but he'd never teased me about my crush on Heath. Never, not once. Why tonight? Was it because of his breakup with Mel? He was hurting, so what, he'd spread the pain? I was his sister, for fuck's sake.

"Asshole," I muttered, refusing to cry.

Heath was never going to be into me. I *knew* Heath was never going to be into me. I'd known for fifteen years. There was no need for Guy to rub it in my face.

Normally after an embarrassing incident, I could avoid Heath for weeks. Months. Not this time. I had to see him on Monday morning. There would be no avoiding this, and now, thanks to Guy's non-existent filter, it would be awkward in the office.

Heath would stare at me with his sparkling gaze and pity me for a silly crush. I didn't want Heath's pity.

"Damn it." A tear dripped free, leaking down my cheek. I brushed it away, walking faster around the corner that would lead me to the parking lot.

"Stella."

I kept my eyes down, my focus on the sidewalk, even though Heath's voice bounced off the downtown buildings.

"Stella, wait."

My legs moved faster.

"Stella." Damn those long legs of his. Heath caught me just before I could open my car door, gripping my elbow and forcing me to stop.

"What?" My voice cracked as I dropped my chin.

"I'm sorry."

"Why?" I shrugged. "It's fine. Just Guy being Guy."

"It's not fine."

No, it wasn't. "Let's forget about it, okay?"

"Stella." That voice. He was making it hard for me not to cry. Because there was pity in his voice. "Look at me."

I shook my head.

He released my elbow, but before I could bolt, he hooked a finger under my chin, tipping my face up to meet his. "Did you really have a crush on me?"

"You know I did," I whispered.

He had to have known. Subtlety had never been one of my talents, especially as a teenager.

"I did know. But I want you to tell me."

"Why? To prolong the humiliation? Can we not talk about this? Please."

"Yeah." He let me go and I spun, reaching for the car, but then he stopped me again by placing a hand beside the window, trapping me between the door and his towering body. "Stella."

"You keep saying my name."

"I love your name."

"I—what?" The tequila had to be messing with me because there was no way I'd heard that right. I twisted to stare up at him and the expression on his face stole my breath.

Not an ounce of pity clouded those blue eyes.

"I think Guy's a prick because it's his way of saying he knows."

"Knows what?"

His eyes searched mine. "That I have a crush on you too."

My mouth fell open.

Which seemed to suit Heath just fine. Because one second he was standing there, staring at my open mouth. The next, his lips covered mine and his tongue slid between my teeth.

CHAPTER FOUR

HEATH

Kissing Stella was not the smartest decision I'd ever made. I mean . . . it was a great fucking move because her lips were the sweetest I'd ever tasted.

But this was Stella.

I'd spent the weekend bouncing from elation to regret and still hadn't decided what to do about it. Pretend it hadn't happened? Tell her it was a mistake? Ask her on a date?

Call in sick so I didn't have to face her today?

"Goddamn it." I rubbed a hand over my jaw, staring at the office building through the windshield of my truck.

Stella was inside already. Her car was parked five down from mine. She'd probably gotten here early, hoping to avoid an awkward encounter in the break room. Or maybe she was packing her things.

Dad was going to kick my ass if I chased away Stella. He'd bragged daily about stealing her from her former company. How she was going to be our new superstar. He wasn't wrong.

And I'd placed her in an uncomfortable situation.

Somehow, I had to make it right. I owed her an apology except I wasn't sorry. Not even a little.

Another truck eased into the space beside mine, and I glanced over to see my brother park and climb out. Time was up. There'd be no more stalling. So I joined him on the snow-dusted sidewalk. "Morning."

"Morning. How was your weekend?"

"Uneventful." Technically, it wasn't a lie since I'd kissed Stella on Friday. My Saturday and Sunday had been spent mostly staring at my living room wall, agonizing over a woman. Questioning the kiss. Fretting about how much I wanted to do it again. "You?"

"I spent most of it here, unburying. I don't want to work all week, especially once Maddox gets here tomorrow."

"I'm hoping to take some vacation too. We should see if he can take a day to ski. It's been a while since the three of us did anything together." Years, actually.

Maddox had moved to California for college and had ended up staying after he'd started his mega-successful streaming network. His company Madcast—and a bitch of an ex-wife—had kept him close to LA in recent years. But he was coming home for the holidays with his daughter, and the last time we'd talked, he'd announced that he was moving home. Finally.

He'd gotten sole custody of his daughter, Violet, after his divorce, and Maddox wanted to raise her closer to family, in the same town where we'd grown up. He wasn't sure of his timeline yet, but it would be good to have him home.

"I could ski," Tobias said, stomping his shoes on the mat inside the door. "Morning, Gretchen."

"Good morning, boys."

With Gretchen, we'd always been *boys*. We always would be boys considering she'd chased us around as toddlers. Gretchen was a staple of Holiday Homes, having worked here longer than any other staff member, except for Dad.

"Morning, Gretchen," I said, keeping my eyes trained forward as I strode down the hallway. I didn't let myself glance upstairs toward Stella's office.

Tobias disappeared into his office and I closed my door.

I'd keep it closed today. I'd stay in my chair, bust out a lot of work so I didn't have to work while Maddox was home. And in doing so, I'd stay on my floor while Stella worked on hers.

I cast my eyes to the ceiling after shrugging off my coat and hanging it on the hook beside the door.

Stella had gasped when I'd kissed her. But she hadn't kissed me back. She'd stood there, frozen, either from shock or December's cold temperatures. When I'd pulled away from her delicious mouth, her eyes had been wide and her cheeks flushed. Then before I could say anything, she gave me a tiny shove away, spun for her car and disappeared.

Why hadn't she kissed me back?

That question had been a plague on my mind. It was what bothered me the most. She'd had a crush on me when we'd been younger, but maybe she'd grown out of it. Maybe I was too damn late.

I sat at my desk. I opened my computer. I stared at the ceiling.

"Stella." I truly loved her name—not something I'd planned on admitting like I had Friday.

Where was her head at? Had she liked the kiss? Hated it?

"Hell." There'd be no work today. Not until I cleared the air. So I blew out a long breath and marched to the second floor.

She was at her desk, one elbow propped on her desk and her chin in her hand. The other was unmoving on her mouse. She stared at the computer screen, unblinking. So lost in thought she hadn't heard me walk down the hall.

"Knock, knock."

She jumped at my voice, the mouse flying out of her hand and across her desk. "H-hi."

"May I come in?"

"Of course." She swallowed hard, stood and wiped her

palms on her jeans. Her long blond hair was down today, the locks curled in loose waves. She was in a chunky sweater that dwarfed her slender form. "What's up?"

I closed the door behind me, then walked to a chair. "May I?"

"Please." She sat too, sitting so straight I was worried she might fall off the edge of her chair.

"About Friday."

"We don't have to talk about it."

"I owe you an apology." The words tasted bitter.

"Okay." She bit her lower lip, worrying it between her teeth as her gaze dropped to her desk.

"I crossed a line. We work together, and I don't want you to think that I'm taking advantage."

She shook her head, a crease forming between her eyebrows. "I don't."

"It won't happen again." Even if I wanted to kiss her again with every cell in my being.

"Yeah, it's, um . . . better to keep things professional."

"Right." Fucking professionalism. "Um . . . how was your weekend?"

Small talk? Really, Holiday? I hated small talk nearly as much as I hated talking about the weather.

"Good." She shrugged. "Boring. You?"

"Same."

Silence settled, heavy and thick. She looked everywhere but at me. The wall. Her keyboard. A coffee mug with a rainbow as the handle.

My apology was out there. I'd done what I'd needed to do. So why was I still in this chair? "Sure is cold out today."

Goddamn it.

"It is." Stella's gaze darted to mine, then flickered away. "Super cold."

Leave. Stand up. Get the hell out of this room. "Are you going to the party?"

"I hadn't planned on it. I was going to go to the Christmas Eve church service with my parents, but then Guy came over yesterday and begged me to be his date."

"Ah." I hadn't spoken to Guy since Friday.

He'd called once on Saturday but I'd ignored him. Mostly because I was pissed that he'd embarrassed Stella. And partly because I wasn't sure if I could face him, knowing that I'd crossed a line.

I loved my best friend, but he could be a bastard. What the fuck had he been thinking, saying that shit to Stell?

She was incredible, and yeah, she'd had a crush. Big deal. A lot of girls in high school had crushed on me.

I'd deal with Guy later. He'd be at my parents' annual Holiday Christmas party on Saturday.

That gave me the week to figure this out.

"You've forgiven him for acting like an ass on Friday?" I asked.

"No. Sort of." Stella lifted a shoulder. "He didn't think it would bother me."

That was bullshit. Guy had said it because he had no filter. Usually his direct declarations would earn a laugh, but this time, he'd gone too far.

"He's pretty upset about his breakup with Mel," she said.

"That doesn't give him an excuse to be a prick."

"I know." She sighed. "I shouldn't defend him, but he's my brother. It's almost Christmas, and I'm picking my battles. I don't want to fight with him, and you know how stubborn he is."

Yes, I did. If Guy didn't see that what he'd done was wrong, he'd hold a grudge and throw a tantrum. It was . . . exhausting. I'd learned to pick my battles too.

"Do you think there will be a good turnout at the party since it's on Christmas Eve?" Stella asked.

"According to Mom's latest RSVP count, most people are coming." Mom and Dad's annual soiree was always a hit with their friends.

"Why is it on Christmas Eve?" Stella asked.

"The Baxter booked out the room for their normal weekend for a wedding. The bride booked it two years ago, but still, Mom was livid. She threatened to move the venue for the rest of time, so the hotel cut her a pretty sweet deal to have it on Christmas Eve."

"I'm glad it worked out."

"Me too."

The silence returned, and I bit my tongue to kill the

small talk. Then I forced myself out of the chair. "I'll let you get back to work."

"Have a good day."

"You too." I lifted a hand to wave, then left her office.

One step into the hallway and I missed the scent of her perfume. But I continued on, returning to my desk and willing Stella from my mind. But did I work? No. I sat in my chair and thought about the beauty on the second floor.

She wanted to keep this professional. Did that mean she regretted the kiss? Did that mean she hadn't kissed me back because of her job? Or because she wasn't attracted to me any longer?

Damn it, I wanted answers. Except this was not the place to discuss it. In the name of *professionalism*, I wouldn't let myself go upstairs again.

My concentration was shot. Maybe I should just pack up my laptop and leave. I could work from home for the week. Or I could work from Mom and Dad's place. Or . . . take vacation time. There was plenty of work to do, but Dad had always encouraged us to take a break when needed.

Today, a break seemed necessary.

"Vacation," I declared and shut my laptop. I'd spend some time away from Stella. Get my head right.

Decision made, I packed what I'd need and grabbed my coat.

"Do you even know what the hell you're doing?" A

man's voice carried down the hallway before I'd stepped out of my office.

I set my stuff aside and rushed out, thinking I was about to see Gretchen put someone in their place. But the question hadn't been aimed at Gretchen. It had been snapped at Stella.

"Mr. Jensen, I apologize." Stella's voice stayed calm and collected. "I understand this is frustrating, but if you want zebrawood for the floors, we will have significant delays in finishing your project."

"Just order it. Express ship it. I don't care. I see no reason why it should take longer. You haven't ordered the white oak yet, right? So just swap it out."

I reached the lobby and caught Gretchen's eye. She nodded to where Stella and Mr. Jensen stood on the opposite side of the space.

Stella had a coffee mug in her hand. Joe Jensen was still wearing his coat. My guess was that Stella had come down for a refill and Joe had caught her in the hall.

"Unfortunately, I can't simply swap it out, Mr. Jensen," Stella said. "Zebrawood is an exotic species and to get the quantity needed will take longer than white oak. The local yard keeps white oak stocked. They don't have any zebrawood."

"Are you sure? Have you asked them?" He leaned forward, bending to talk in her face.

That move right there pissed me right the fuck off. Yes,

he was a client, but there was no reason for him to attempt to intimidate her.

Not that his attempt worked.

Stella stood taller and plastered on a fake smile. "No, you're right. I haven't asked them. But I'll make a call right now. If you're sure that's what you want, I'll get a change order and new project schedule to you by this afternoon."

"Yes, that's what I want." He backed away, his lips pursed. Then Joe spotted me and walked right past Stella, nearly bumping his shoulder against hers. He was all smiles as he crossed the lobby, his hand extended. "Heath. How's it going? Do you have a minute?"

"Hi, Joe. Happy holidays. And for you, sure." I nodded toward the nearest conference room. "Have a seat. I'll meet you in there."

"Fantastic." He unzipped his coat as he passed me by.

Joe was going to ask me to take on his project. I didn't have to set foot in the conference room to know exactly what this conversation would entail. But Joe was about to be disappointed.

Stella's shoulders fell as she turned and walked for the stairs, her gaze glued to the floor. She knew what Joe was about to ask me too.

An hour later, I escorted Joe from the conference room. He wasn't entirely happy that I'd refused to take his build on myself, but after a lengthy discussion, he understood that if he wanted the project done right, he needed Stella.

"Thanks, Heath."

"Sure." I nodded, escorting him to the lobby. "See you at the party Saturday?"

"Wouldn't miss it." He waved at Gretchen, then pushed out the door.

Gretchen watched him leave, tracking his steps until he was in his Cadillac, then she shook her head. "I've never liked Joe. Today just reinforced my opinion. The way he marched in here and practically jumped on Stella. He didn't even tell her hello."

"He's . . . difficult."

"Understatement," Gretchen muttered.

My plan to leave and avoid Stella had been shattered, so I headed for the stairs.

She sat behind her desk, her fingers moving furiously over the keyboard as she glared at her monitor. The *click, click, click* was so loud that I didn't bother knocking.

"Hey."

"Hi." Her eyes darted to mine, but her fingers never stopped. "Zebrawood will take an additional six months to arrive. It's back-ordered and has been for months. For an order this size, and with the lumberyard's specialty wood stocking fee, I hope Joe's got his checkbook ready because this is going to cost him."

I rounded the corner of her desk, propping up on the edge as her fingers continued their assault on the keys. "Hey."

She typed a few more words, then paused, glancing up. "Did he ask for someone else to run his project?"

"Yes."

Her hands dropped to her lap, her chin to her chest. "I figured as much. The first assignment from your dad too."

"I told him no."

Her face whirled to mine. "You did?"

"He's abrasive and arrogant."

"Don't forget condescending."

"He's all those things, Stell. But he's also logical. He wants this job done and he realizes that to make that happen, he's got to make certain decisions. You told him *no*, which is not something he's heard yet with this project. But you stood up for yourself. He respects that. He told me the same just before he left."

"Your dad is testing me with this one, isn't he?"

I chuckled. "Yep."

"Thank you for not pulling me off it. Joe and I might not end this as friends, but I'll do a good job."

"I know you will."

"Just keep rolling with the kicks, right?"

"Um . . . what?" I replayed that sentence in my head. Roll with the kicks? "You mean roll with the punches. That's the saying."

"Maybe but it's a dumb saying. If someone kicks me, guaranteed I'm dropping to the floor. And then if they keep trying to kick me, I'll just roll away."

I blinked. "Rolling with the punches is an expression from boxing. You roll with a punch to lessen the impact."

"But I'm not a boxer. So rolling with the kicks makes more sense."

"Does it?"

"Yes."

I studied her beautiful face. "No."

"Well . . ." She shrugged. "Disagree to agree."

This woman. Somehow, her nonsense made sense.

As her hazel eyes locked with mine, I realized just how close we were. Almost as close as we'd been on Friday before I'd kissed her.

All I had to do was lean down. All she had to do was shift six inches.

Stella Marten was as tempting as a wrapped gift under the Christmas tree.

But she hadn't kissed me back.

So I moved, standing from her desk and putting it between us. "I'm sorry. About Joe. And Friday."

She nodded, her shoulders turning in on themselves. "It's fine."

It wasn't okay. Because all I could think about was doing it again. "I, um . . . I'd better get going."

I had a vacation to start. A very necessary vacation. "Bye, Stell."

With my feet aimed for the door, I was just about to the safety of the hallway when she called my name.

"Heath?"

I turned, putting a hand on the door's frame. Maybe if I held on tight enough, it would keep me on this side of the room. "Yeah?"

"Why did you kiss me?"

I answered her question with one of my own. "Do you still have a crush on me?"

Because if it was over, if it was something she'd let go along with her adolescence, then I'd stop this. Somehow, I'd stop thinking about her.

"We work together." Her answer was like a knife to the heart. "You're Guy's best friend."

"Right." I swallowed my disappointment. "We should keep this professional."

"We should." She nodded. "That's a good—smart —idea."

It was a fucking horrible idea. But I'd respect her wishes. "I'll see you at the party."

"Oh, you're not working this week?"

"Maddox is coming home. I'm taking a vacation."

A Stella vacation.

And maybe by Saturday, I'd have forgotten the taste of her on my tongue.

CHAPTER FIVE

STELLA

"You look hot." Wendy whistled. "Smoking hot."

"That's a lot of eye shadow." I picked up a blending brush, but Wendy slapped it from my hand.

"Don't even think about ruining my masterpiece."

My shoulders slumped as I stared at myself in the mirror. "I don't want to go."

"Why not? I thought you were excited."

"Headache," I lied.

The truth was mine and mine alone. Wendy was my best friend, but I was taking Heath's kiss to the grave. Well . . . maybe not the grave. Keeping secrets was not my forte and the only reason I'd managed so far was that Wendy and I had both been busy.

Tonight was the first time I'd seen her all week, and from the moment she'd walked through the door, we'd focused solely on getting me ready for this party.

A party I didn't want to attend. Not with my brother. And not with Heath.

I still wasn't sure what to think about that kiss. Mostly, I tried not to think about it because the shame that came with that memory—a memory I should have cherished—made me want to curl up in a ball and hide under my bed for the next twenty years.

My only saving grace had been Heath's absence from the office. Never in my life had I looked forward to *not* seeing Heath, but his vacation had been my reprieve.

A reprieve that ended tonight.

"After a couple drinks, I bet you'll feel better." Wendy gave me a soft smile in the mirror.

"Yeah." I smiled back. "Thanks for helping me get ready."

"What are best friends for? I have to live vicariously through you. I can't remember the last time I had an excuse to get dolled up and wear a sexy dress."

"But you get to wear leggings every day. I'd trade leggings for a sexy dress any time."

"This is true." She laughed. "Okay, what shoes?"

"Nude heels?"

"Agreed. I'll grab them."

As she rushed from the bathroom, I twirled the skirt of my dress, feeling the swish of the fabric over my legs.

The top had a plunging neckline that dipped low enough to be sexy but not too low to be scandalous. This was technically a work function. The flowing skirt hit me midcalf with a slit on one end that ran to my thigh. The dress was black with a deep plum overlay adorned with sparkles. My hair was curled. My hazel eyes were lined with black and shadowed in gray.

Wendy was right. I did look hot. A year ago, I would have done all this and more, just in the hope of snagging Heath's attention. Tonight, I wanted to wash it all away simply to blend in with the crowd.

He'd kissed me. Heath Holiday had kissed me.

And he'd regretted it.

I squeezed my eyes shut, willing the pained look on his face from Monday out of my head.

Heath's lips had been so soft. So delicious. One sweep of his tongue across mine and I'd about fainted. How long had I wanted a kiss? How long had I hoped for Heath's?

My one chance and I'd blown it.

He'd kissed me and I'd stood there like a dumbstruck fool. Mouth hanging open. Drool pooling.

That kiss had been a sheer disaster. The equivalent of a Christmas tree catching fire. Suggesting we keep things professional had been my last-ditch attempt to save face.

The worst part? I was a good kisser. I was a really good kisser. I'd had boyfriends who'd told me the same. So why, when presented the one and only opportunity to kiss Heath Holiday, had I failed so epically?

"Damn you, stage fright."

"What?" Wendy came into the bathroom carrying my strappy nude heels.

"Oh. Nothing." I took the shoes, bending to put them on and secure the strap at my ankles. They weren't exactly practical for a December night, but fashion required sacrifice. And frostbite risk. "Thanks."

"Do me a favor. Try to have fun tonight. I know it's always interesting with your brother around, but ditch him and enjoy the party. It's your Christmas Eve too."

"Okay." I pulled her into a hug. "Merry Christmas."

"Merry Christmas."

The doorbell chimed, sending us out of the bedroom in a flurry. Wendy rushed to collect the makeup she'd brought over while I grabbed my coat and clutch.

"Hi, Guy," she said, opening the door before pushing past him. "Bye, Guy."

His lip curled. "Wendy."

My brother and my best friend had never gotten along. Guy thought Wendy was a snob because she never laughed at his jokes. Wendy thought he was self-absorbed and crass—hence the reason she didn't laugh with Guy.

I'd stopped playing mediator years ago.

"You look very pretty, Stella Bells." He took my coat and held it out. "You'll be the most beautiful girl at the party."

"Thanks." I slid my arms in. "You look nice too. New suit?"

"It is. I thought it was time for an upgrade." He offered me his arm. "Ready for this?"

No. I blew out a long breath. "Ready."

"Thanks for coming with me tonight."

"You're welcome." I bumped my shoulder to his. "Sorry about Mel."

"Me too." He gave me a sad smile. "I liked her."

"Want to talk about it?"

"Not tonight. Let's just have fun. Me and you. I get all your dances."

I nodded. "Deal."

The cold night air was brittle on the bare skin of my calves as we hurried to his truck. But he'd left the engine running and the seat warmers on.

"How was work this week?" he asked as he eased out of the parking lot.

"Good. Great, actually. I feel like I'm settling in and I like it so far."

"They're lucky to have you."

"Thanks."

"So what have you been working on?"

I spent the drive downtown telling him about my projects. Guy had spent a lot of years tuning me out—little sisters were probably annoying at times. I'd spent a lot of years ignoring my big brother too. But he listened as he drove and asked a few questions, engaged in what I had to say.

I'd been dreading tonight, not only because of Heath but because Guy had the habit of ditching me. He'd get around his friends and I'd become an afterthought. But maybe tonight would be different. Maybe he'd stick with me and we could have a good time.

Guy could be my savior. The buffer between Heath and me. There was no way Heath would mention that kiss while my brother was around. And I really, really didn't want to hear another apology.

"Want me to drop you off at the door?" Guy asked as we reached The Baxter.

"No, that's okay. I can walk."

"But you're in sandals. Your toes are going to get cold."

"It's fine." I wanted to know where the car was in case he had a few too many cocktails and I needed to drive us home.

"Suit yourself." He shrugged and circled the block, finding the closest spot available.

Guy lent me his arm as we hurried down the sidewalk, the streetlights on Main glowing brighter as we reached the hotel.

The Baxter, like the other buildings downtown, was magical over the holidays. Through the golden and glass doors, the lobby was the picture of holiday festivities. Even on Christmas Eve, the space was bustling with people. Some were here to dine at a restaurant on the main floor. Some were here for drinking. A group was clustered around the bar in the corner, each holding a fancy cocktail.

A couple stood beneath a sprig of mistletoe and shared a kiss. In the corner was a massive tree, its bows adorned with lights and ornaments. A few kids were hovering over a bowl of candy canes.

Guy led us straight for the grand, sweeping staircase that led to the ballroom on the second floor. "Can I put the keys in your purse?"

"Sure." I opened it for him as we ascended the stairs, stopping by the coat check. Then, with my jacket and clutch tagged and stowed, we walked into the ballroom.

Conversation floated above the background music. Caterers swept through the room, passing from person to person with trays of hors d'oeuvres. Two bartenders, each wearing white shirts and black satin vests, mixed drinks at the bar.

Keith stood next to his wife, Hannah, both welcoming us as we came into the room. I tried my very hardest, but my eyes scanned the crowd, searching for Heath. Old habits.

He wasn't here yet.

"Drink?" Guy asked.

"Please." I nodded, smiling at a few familiar faces as we walked toward the bar.

Gretchen waved from her spot at a cocktail table. A few others from the office were huddled together with their spouses.

Joe Jensen stood at another table, nodding when I met his gaze. I smiled too wide at the asshole. Last week after our encounter in the office, I'd emailed him the updated flooring estimates.

He had yet to respond.

The ballroom was decked out for the party. An empty stage was prepped and waiting for a live band. The tall tables were covered with pressed white linens and each had a tiny bouquet of red roses in its center. The room's crystal chandelier cast a twinkling glow over the empty dance floor.

"What do you want?" Guy asked as we waited in line at the bar.

"Champagne." I'd have a headache tomorrow, not ideal for Christmas Day, but this party and this room demanded a drink with bubbles.

With my flute in hand, Guy and I headed for a table.

"Cheers." He clinked his vodka tonic with my glass.

"Cheers." I took a sip and scanned the room again, my gaze landing on the doorway just as Heath walked in.

My heart skipped. Wow, he looked good.

His black suit accentuated his broad shoulders. His dark hair was parted on one side and styled with a swoop above his eyebrow. The tie he wore was a blue nearly as bright as the color of his eyes.

No man was as handsome as Heath. Movie stars. Professional athletes. Models. I'd let other women drool over them because Heath outshone them all, inside and out.

Maybe that was why it was so hard to let go of this crush. Because the man himself was unforgettable. He was good and kind and charming. He stood apart from every other face in the crowd, demanding attention. That chiseled jaw. The straight nose. The full lips. My mouth went dry so I took another drink.

Heath spotted us and smiled. A smile so dazzling, I choked.

Coughing and snorting, I somehow managed to swallow and not spew champagne over the table.

"Jesus." Guy patted my back. "Are you okay?"

I waved him off. "Fine. Wrong pipe."

He gave me a sideways look, but when he spotted his best friend walking our way, my near-death incident was forgotten. "Finally. Heath's coming over. Now the party can start."

"Gee, thanks," I muttered.

"You know what I mean."

"Do I?"

Guy shrugged and reached into his suit jacket pocket for a piece of spearmint gum. He almost always chewed gum because he never wanted bad breath if there was—in his words—*a hot chick around who wanted to suck face.*

A poet, my brother.

"About time you got here." Guy clapped Heath on the shoulder as he joined us.

"Hey." Heath shook my brother's hand. "Hi, Stell."

"Hi." I raised my champagne flute to my lips, drinking more carefully this time, and doing everything in my power not to stare. The flowers on the table really were beautiful.

"So, what's the plan of attack?" Guy asked Heath. "Maybe have a few drinks. Dance. Then find a woman to entertain. I do love seeing a sexy dress on my bedroom floor."

I scrunched up my nose. "Please stop talking."

"Kidding." Guy laughed, but we all knew he wasn't joking. I had no doubt that it was rare for either Guy or Heath to leave this party alone. The image of Heath with another woman made my skin crawl.

"Let's just enjoy the party," Heath said, giving me a strained smile.

Awkward. I swallowed a groan.

This wasn't even my fault. I'd been the catalyst for plenty of embarrassing moments, but this one was all Heath. *He'd* kissed *me*. Yes, I could have done a much better job at kissing him, but this wasn't my fault. I did not instigate the kissing.

Why was it that a man could kiss a woman and completely forget it, but a woman would analyze every single second? Or maybe that was just me? I'd likely analyze Heath's kiss for the rest of my life. That really, truly, horrendously amazing kiss.

"Surprised you didn't beat us here," Guy told him.

"I rode with Maddox and Violet." Heath hooked his thumb over his shoulder to where his brother strolled into the room with an adorable little girl at his side and a stunning woman trailing behind them.

I did a double take. Not at Maddox, but at the woman and her friendly face.

"Excuse me." I set my flute down and made my way to my friend. "Nat!"

Her face lit up when she spotted me. "Hey, Stella."

"It's so good to see you." I hugged her, wishing we saw each other more.

Natalie was two years older, the same age as Guy and Heath. She'd been a junior when I'd joined the high school swim team as a freshman. Even though I'd been younger and possessed only a fraction of her talent in the pool, she'd always cheered for me. She'd never treated me like I was beneath her.

Unlike Guy and Heath, Natalie hadn't been in the popular crowd at Bozeman High, and I'd always looked up to her because of her kind heart.

We'd stayed in touch over the years since neither of us had left Bozeman after graduation. She'd started working as a nanny while I'd gone straight to Montana State for my bachelor's degree.

"I had no idea you'd be here," I said. But her presence settled some nerves. Wait. Was she here with Maddox? Were they dating?

"It was a last-minute invite. I'm actually here to work."

The young girl she'd come in with appeared at her side. This had to be Maddox's daughter. She had his dark hair and blue eyes. Without so much as a glance my way, she held up an empty punch cup to Natalie. "Can I have more?"

"Let's pace ourselves. We have all night." Natalie laughed, looking back at me.

"How are you?" I asked. "It's been forever."

She opened her mouth to answer, but Guy appeared at my side along with Heath.

Guy was talking, but the moment he spotted Natalie he did his own double take. "Natalie?"

"Hey. Good to see you, Guy."

"Been a while." My brother's jaw worked as he chewed that gum. And checked out her ass.

I rolled my eyes. Seriously, he'd just gone through a breakup. *Men.*

"Guy." Natalie shook her head when he looked up and met her gaze.

"You sure?"

She giggled. "Quite. But thanks anyway."

He chuckled. "Are you here alone?"

"Nope." She waved to the girl. "Violet's my date tonight. And we're raiding the dessert table before any of the good stuff disappears."

"Natalie's the coolest of the cool," I told Violet. "You're going to have a blast tonight."

"But not as cool as Uncle Heath, right?" Heath held out his hand for Violet to smack it.

She blinked and ignored him.

"Ouch." Heath feigned a wound to the heart.

I giggled. I should have ignored him, but I couldn't help it. I'd spent years laughing whenever Heath made a joke. Another old habit that refused to die, along with the blush that crept up my cheeks when he made eye contact.

His gaze dipped to the low-cut neckline of my dress and for a moment, my heart fluttered. But then he tore his eyes away, guilt creeping into his expression.

Ugh. I really should have stayed home in my sweatpants.

"Be my wingman." Guy nudged Heath's arm, jerking his chin to the door. I followed my brother's gaze to where a petite blonde and pretty brunette had just entered the room. "Hit on the blonde."

Oh, God. I dropped my face to my nude heels. I was going to have to stay here and watch while Heath picked up another woman. He'd said before the kiss that he'd had a crush on me. But I guess my non-kiss had squashed it.

Champagne. What I needed right now was more champagne.

"Um . . ." Heath trailed off as Guy hauled him away.

Unlike me, I bet that blonde would kiss him back if given the chance.

It shouldn't hurt. I was over my crush, right? So why did it hurt so much? How many hurts would it take to finally give this up?

"You okay?" Natalie bumped her elbow with mine.

"Great!" *Too loud.* I cringed at the volume of my voice.

"I didn't know you'd be here tonight," she said.

"I just started working at Holiday Homes. Keith invites the whole office. I was actually going to skip and go to church with my parents, then hang out at home, but Guy talked me into coming."

I should have known better. We'd been here for minutes and I was already getting left behind.

"He promised to hang out with me because his girl-friend just dumped him," I said. "He's kind of broken up about it, even though he won't admit it. I felt bad for him, so I told him I'd be his date. But . . . he just ditched me."

"Want to hang with us?"

"I think I'm going to grab a drink." Drinks, to be accurate. Multiple drinks. And after drinking the multiple drinks, I'd call an Uber or Wendy to drive me home.

Natalie waved, taking Violet to the dessert table, while I headed toward the bar. I didn't want to see him talking and laughing with another woman, so I kept my chin down, eyes on the floor.

So focused on *not* watching for Heath, I nearly stumbled when I lifted my gaze and there he was. My footsteps stuttered. "H-hi."

"Hi. Can I buy you a drink?" he asked, nodding to the bar.

"Oh, um . . . you're not getting one for the, uh . . ." My fingers flittered over my shoulder in the direction of the door.

"No. Guy's on his own tonight."

I glanced behind me to where my brother was talking to the brunette. The blonde was nowhere in sight.

"What do you say, Stell? How about a drink?" There was pleading in his eyes. Maybe if this was just us at the office, him in jeans and a button-down, I would have had the strength to say no. But damn it, he looked so sexy in that suit. It was his fault that my resolve crumbled.

"Sure," I breathed.

His hypnotic eyes sparkled as we shuffled into the line at the bar.

"Do you still keep in touch with Natalie?" he asked.

A man beside me moved too close, accidentally bumping my shoulder with his.

Heath's hand drifted to the small of my back to steady me. Except when the man apologized and inched away, Heath's hand stayed. What the hell? What was happening?

I swallowed hard, trying to remember the question he'd asked. Nope. Nothing. My mind was blank. "Huh?"

"Natalie." He chuckled. "Do you keep in touch with her?"

"Oh. Yes." I nodded. "We meet for drinks two or three times a year. We gossip about people we knew from high school and she tells me about the kids she's watching."

"Then your next meetup should be entertaining since she's nannying Violet." He laughed. "That kid is a handful. Earlier this week, Maddox found her with a butcher's knife in the kitchen. She was going to cut herself a piece of apple pie."

"Seriously?" I giggled.

"It gets better." As we inched forward, he told me story after story about Violet's antics, some from this week and others he'd heard secondhand from his mom.

"She sounds . . . entertaining."

"I think we should put Violet and Guy together. We'd be guaranteed a show."

"Probably not tonight," I said. "There are a lot of breakables in this room."

"Good call." He winked as we finally reached the bar. With a whiskey tumbler in his hand and another champagne flute in mine, we turned to leave.

Heath's hand went to the small of my back again, but as we stepped out of the line, Gretchen appeared. His hand dropped and he slid away. "Gretchen."

"Hi, handsome." She gave him a hug. "Say, I need a few. There's a client who wanted to have a quick chat."

"Tonight?" He groaned.

"No such thing as a day off," she said.

"Right." Heath sighed. "See you later, Stella."

"Bye." I raised my flute.

I stared as Gretchen weaved through the crowd with Heath not far behind. Then I glanced around and realized I was alone.

My brother had vanished. Typical. Natalie was with Violet by the dessert table, and though I was sure she wouldn't care if I hung out with her tonight, I didn't want to intrude since she was working.

So I inched closer to the wall, wishing I could blend in with the wallpaper.

The lead singer of the live band took the microphone, welcoming the guests. Then with his band in position, they kicked off their show with a sultry jazz number that drew couples to the dance floor.

I listened to them perform, drinking my champagne. The bubbly went down too smoothly, and before the band's first set was over, I was three flutes in. My head was beautifully buzzed. My bruised heart coated in delicious bubbles. One more glass, then I'd find a quick bite to eat before sneaking out the door.

With my empty flute in hand, I left the safety of the wall to get in line at the bar. I'd just joined the queue when a man appeared at my side.

His dirty-blond hair was short and neatly combed. His charcoal suit was stylish and tailored to his lean frame. He was cute too. Really cute. Not Heath handsome, but no one was Heath handsome, not even Tobias.

"Hi." He held out his hand.

"Hi."

"I'm Seth."

"Stella," I said, sliding my palm against his.

"Beautiful name."

I smiled. "Thank you."

"Forgive me if this is too forward." He nodded to the dance floor. "But would you like to dance?"

"Um . . ." Why the hell not? "I'd love to."

He offered me his arm and together we navigated the crowd, settling at the edge of the dance floor. His cologne wafted to my nose as he spun me into his arms, one hand taking mine as the other settled on the curve of my hip.

Seth pulled us together, not too close, not too distant. And then we danced, stepping and turning in our own little square. "I'm not the best dancer in the world."

"You're doing great." A new blush crept into my face at the interest in his gaze.

He had dark brown eyes. Attractive, though not Heath's mesmerizing color. Seth's shoulders weren't as broad and his frame wasn't as tall.

What the hell was wrong with me? Here I was dancing with a handsome man who actually wanted me, and I kept comparing him to Heath. This had to stop. Right now. *Stop it, Stella.*

"So how do you know the Holidays?" Seth asked.

"I work at Holiday Homes. You?"

"I'm a realtor at Hannah's firm."

"Ah." I nodded.

"Maybe we'll get to work together on a project one of these days."

"Maybe."

Since Keith was the premier builder in the valley and Hannah owned one of the largest brokerages, often her realtors would meet with buyers who couldn't find a home on the market and instead, they'd decide to build. We'd collaborate on the property and the handoff to get the customer their dream home.

Or so I'd been told. I hadn't had the chance to do one of those projects yet.

"Are you from Bozeman?" he asked.

"I am. Born and raised. You?"

Before Seth could answer, a towering figure appeared at our side. I looked up to find a pair of very blue, very angry eyes, locked on Seth's hand at my waist.

"Stella." Heath's jaw clenched. "May I speak with you for a minute? Work related. You understand."

"Uh . . ." Seth didn't get the chance to finish that sentence.

Heath's hand wrapped around my elbow and he all but dragged me off the dance floor.

"Heath," I hissed when a few people gave us a sideways look.

He didn't slow.

"Heath." I yanked my arm free, forcing him to stop.

He turned, giving me a warning glare, then his hand was back, this time engulfing mine as he led me through the ballroom. He strode out the doors and down the hallway, shoving through the first door we reached.

We stepped into a sitting room. Couches hugged the far wall. A plush chair sat angled into a corner.

Heath let me go and strode into the center of the space, dragging a hand through his hair.

"What's going on?"

He turned and held up a finger to my nose. "You."

"What about me? What's wrong?"

"You . . ." He tipped his head to the ceiling and blew out a long breath. As his lungs emptied, the tension faded from his face. "You look beautiful."

"I—oh." Okay, not what I was expecting. "Thank you?"

"No." He leveled me with that gaze. "Don't say thank you. Just stop."

"Stop what?"

He stepped close, too close. As close as he'd been that night beside my car. "Stop being beautiful. Stop dancing with other men. Just for tonight. Don't dance with that guy. I'm trying to respect your wishes here, Stella. But tonight, it's a struggle."

"My wishes? What wishes?"

"To keep this professional." He sneered as he spoke the last word.

"That was your idea. Not mine."

"Was it?" He arched an eyebrow. "Because I clearly remember it being your suggestion."

Yes, it had been. I'd only suggested it to salvage a tiny shred of my pride. "You came into my office and apologized for kissing me."

"I apologized because you didn't kiss me back."

"I—" *Oh. My. God.* He thought I didn't want him. "I was just surprised."

He studied my face. "What do you want? Tell me what you want."

I wanted what I'd always wanted. "You. I want—"

He cut me off by slamming his mouth on mine.

It took me a heartbeat. Maybe I'd never truly get over the shock of Heath's lips. But I recovered.

And this time, I kissed him back.

CHAPTER SIX

HEATH

J ust one more kiss. Then I'd stop. That had been the
plan.

But the moment Stella's tongue slid against
mine, I lost any hope of restraint. The truth was, I'd lost it
the moment I'd seen her dancing with another man.

"Stella," I moaned, cupping her face in my hands.

She clung to me, her tongue tangling with mine, and
goddamn it, she could kiss.

Stella could fucking *kiss*.

No reluctance. No shock or restraint. This was not the
same woman who I'd kissed last weekend beside her car.

I devoured her, and she met me beat for beat.

Her lips moved frantically over mine as my hands
roamed over her shoulders, following the curve of her
spine. Like I'd cupped her face, I fit my palms over her ass.
Then I squeezed. But I didn't linger. I traced her hips,

then her ribs, wanting to feel every inch of this woman. I wanted to lose myself in her slender curves and sweet taste.

My tongue dueled with hers as I banded my arms around her, pulling her flush against my chest. When my growing arousal dug into her hip, she gasped, and that adorable little hitch in her breath only made me want her more.

I tore my mouth away from hers, wanting to taste her skin. As my lips trailed down the long column of her throat, Stella's fingers dove into my hair, threading through the strands. One tug and I was hard as a rock.

She arched her back and I dropped lower, pulling aside the fabric of her dress to reveal a perfect breast. No bra. *Thank fuck.*

A rosy nipple popped free and I didn't hesitate to suck it into my mouth.

"Heath," she whimpered.

I nipped and lapped at the bud until Stella moaned my name again. Her skin was so smooth. Her breast was the perfect swell to fit the cup of my hand. I was just about to move to the other side when the door to the sitting room swung open.

"Oh my God," a woman squeaked. "I'm sorry."

Stella gasped, shoving at my shoulders.

I glanced over my shoulder as Stella scrambled to right her dress. "Natalie?"

"Heath?"

Natalie glanced between the two of us, her eyes wide. "I wasn't here. I didn't see anything. You two, um, have fun."

There was a smirk on Nat's lips as she slipped out of the room, leaving Stella and me alone.

My breath came in labored pants. Stella's face was beautifully flushed and her pink mouth swollen. God, I could kiss her for years if it meant that color was mine and mine alone.

I dragged a hand through my hair and inspected the door. No lock. Damn it. I was teetering on the edge of control, but I didn't need another person walking in on us —like her brother—so I took a step away.

Stella cleared her throat and smoothed down the skirt of her dress.

This was wrong. So, so wrong. My reasons for not chasing Stella hadn't changed in the last week. Nothing had changed. Yet everything had changed.

Seeing her with that guy on the dance floor had felt like a lightning rod piercing my heart. No woman had ever made me feel so jealous. The only man she'd be dancing with tonight was me.

"Heath, I . . ." She put her hands on her cheeks. "What are we doing?"

I stepped closer, pulling her hands away. "Don't hide from me."

She looked up to me and those expressive eyes were so full of uncertainty it made my chest ache. "I don't know what you want. That's fairly terrifying for me because the one thing I've always wanted was you."

Stella spoke like those words had been waiting a week, a year, to make their way free. The vulnerability in her voice was humbling.

"I meant what I said the other night. Stell, I've wanted you for a long time."

"Really?"

"Longer than I would let myself admit."

She pulled her lower lip between her teeth to hide a shy smile.

I put my thumb on that lip to tug it free. "We should stop."

"No." She shook her head. "We should leave."

"Together?"

She nodded and let out a rushed breath. "But you should know I used it up."

"Used what up?"

"My champagne bravery." She tucked a lock of hair behind her ear. "I just told you that I've always wanted you. That used up all of my bravery. So now you have to take charge because I'm too busy having a mental freak-out that you just kissed me and sucked one of my nipples and said that you want me too, and oh my God, you want me too? How is this even happ—"

"Breathe, baby."

She obeyed, nodding as she dragged in some air.

"Better?"

"Yes."

"Good." I leaned forward and kissed her forehead, then took her hand in mine and dragged her out of the sitting room.

Our first stop was at the coat check. After we got her jacket and clutch, she checked Guy's keys under his name while I ordered us an Uber. As soon as we had her belongings, I rushed her down the staircase and into the winter night.

Snow was falling lightly as we slid into the backseat of a black sedan. The icy flakes melted instantly on the car's windshield. Even over the smell of air freshener and leather, Stella's sweet scent filled my nose.

The driver confirmed my address and that was the last shred of attention he earned. I focused entirely on Stella, drawing in her perfume, holding it for a heartbeat, before leaning in close for a deeper inhale.

We were only blocks away from The Baxter when I buried my nose in her curled tresses, pulling her hair away from her shoulder so I could duck down to kiss her throat.

The moment my lips hit her pulse, her breath hitched. Shy. Sexy. The sound shot straight to my cock. I'd earn a hundred of those tonight if she had them to give.

"Stella," I whispered against her skin.

Her hand came up, cupping the back of my head and holding me in place.

I grinned and peppered the delicate spot beneath her

ear with open-mouthed kisses until her fingers dug into my scalp.

Other than my mouth, I didn't dare touch her. I didn't trust myself not to take her in the back of this car, damn the driver watching through the rearview mirror.

Traffic was light and by the time we stopped in front of my house, my dick was aching. Stella unbuckled her seat belt first, practically shoving me out of the car. Then we raced up the sidewalk to my front door.

The moment I had the key in the lock, Stella reached beneath the hem of my suit coat and slid her hands up the plane of my back. I leaned into the touch, forgetting for a second that we were outside. That the snow was falling and catching the white glow of the Christmas lights I'd strung on the eaves.

"Are we going inside?" she asked.

I answered by twisting the lock and stepping inside with Stella on my heels. Then I kicked the door shut before sealing my lips over hers.

She rose on her toes, twisted her tongue against mine as I banded my arms around her and hauled her to my chest. When I shuffled toward the nearest wall of the entryway and hoisted her up, she wrapped her legs around my waist, pressing her center into my erection.

Stella might have told me to take control, but I was following her lead. She nipped and I sucked, tasting every corner of her mouth. One of her hands slipped between us, her fingers searching for my belt buckle.

I tore my mouth away, gritting my teeth. I ached for her, but when we crossed this line, there was no going back. "Stella, be sure."

She lifted her hand free and brought it to my forehead, pushing the hair away. "I'm sure."

"This changes everything."

"I think that we've already changed everything, don't you?"

"Yeah," I whispered, drowning in her gaze. "I guess we have."

She leaned in, pressing her lips to the corner of my mouth as she tilted her hips forward, urging me on.

Maybe she hadn't used all that bravery. Or maybe she had more courage than she let herself believe, champagne or not. Timid or bold, I'd take her in every way.

Her fingers found the clasp on my belt and began to tug.

"Wait." I pulled away, panting. "We're not doing this against the wall."

"No?"

I shook my head. "No."

She moved to let her legs down but I swept her away, earning a little laugh as I carried her out of the entryway. Every room was dark, the only light coming from the Christmas tree in the corner. Its multicolored bulbs cast their red, blue, green and yellow light over the living room.

If Stella was curious about my home, she didn't let on. She didn't look away from my face or loosen her hold on my shoulders as I strode down the long hallway to my bedroom.

Like the living room, I'd put a small tree in a corner. Maybe other men wouldn't bother with decorations, considering there were no family gatherings planned for my place, but I loved Christmas and falling asleep to the glow of the lighted tree.

Stella unwrapped her legs as I set her on the foot of the bed. She reached for me but I shook my head and dropped to my knees. My hands were trembling.

When was the last time I'd been anxious with a woman? Maybe my first time? That had been in high school, after prom. Even then, we'd each had enough cheap liquor to chase away the nerves.

This was Stella.

My fingers fumbled with the straps on her shoes. I willed my heart to stop racing. When her hands came to my hair again, I leaned into her touch and closed my eyes.

"I can't believe this is happening." Her confession was barely audible. The honesty in her voice, the heart shining through those dazzling eyes, was my undoing. There was no woman as beautiful as Stella Marten.

And I'd been a coward for too long. A fool for not acting sooner.

Now she was fucking mine.

When I went back to her heels, the shaking in my fingers was gone. If all I did tonight was make this good for her, I'd call it a win. I plucked her shoes from her feet, tossing them aside, then trailed my fingers across the smooth skin on her ankle, working my way toward the inside of her knee.

My fingertips moved in slow, torturous swirls, never leaving her skin as I inched along her legs. A shiver shook her shoulders as I brushed the skirt of her dress across her thighs, pushing it higher and higher. Her breath hitched again, that sexy-as-fuck gasp, when I skimmed her hips and along the lace of her panties.

Her eyes were hooded when I met her gaze, her bottom lip between her teeth again.

I gave her a smirk as I balled her dress in my fists and dragged it up her torso. She raised her arms as I whipped it free.

"You are . . ." My mouth went dry at the image of her on my bed, naked but for those panties. "Perfect. My Stella. So fucking perfect."

Even in the muted light, I saw the pink blush of her cheeks.

I took her face in my hands, pulling her to my mouth. Then I stood, not loosening my hold, as I laid her on the mattress.

The ministrations I'd done with my hands I now did with my mouth, trailing open-mouthed kisses across her neck and down her chest, stopping to pay her nipples more attention. Then I moved lower, dragging my tongue around her navel.

She whimpered, a sound I was beginning to love as much as that gasp.

I lingered above the hem of her panties, dragging in her sweet scent as I tucked my fingers into the lace and dragged them away from her bare mound.

"Heath." Stella gulped the moment the fabric was free, pooled on the floor beside her dress and heels. "I've, um, no one has ever . . . I mean, I'm not a virgin but, uh, you know."

Oh. Fuck. Me.

I'd be the first to taste her. The only. My mouth watered. "Do you trust me?"

She nodded.

"Good." I pressed at her knees, spreading them apart.

Her folds glistened, her pussy as pretty a pink as her lips. Her muscles tightened, her legs tense. It would be fun to tease her one of these days. To kiss everywhere but where she needed it. But for our first time, I didn't delay.

I dragged my tongue through her slit, moaning at her taste.

Stella let out a little cry, slapping a hand over her mouth.

I chuckled, licking her again.

"Oh my God." It was muffled from beneath her hand, but I was taking it as approval to devour.

I lapped at her, sucking her clit into my mouth, taking her to the edge, over and over. When her legs were shaking, her body writhing, I'd back off.

By the fifth time, the hand on her mouth was gone, and her hands fisted the charcoal comforter. By the tenth, she was growling in frustration.

"Want to come, baby?" I asked.

"Yes."

"Your wish, Stell." This time, I didn't back off. I kept at her until her back arched off the bed, her entire body spasming as she let out a string of moans. Only when her toes uncurled did I stop.

Her chest was rosy, her body limp.

I licked my lips and stood, shrugging off my suit coat as I memorized the image of a naked Stella on my bed. My cock was painfully hard, the bulge straining at the zipper on my slacks. I made short work of undressing, and when my clothes were strewn beside hers, I gripped my shaft and gave it a hard stroke.

"I haven't been with anyone for a while," I said. "And I had a checkup last month."

Stella nodded frantically. "Me neither. And I'm on the pill."

This night just kept getting better. I planted a knee on the bed, picking her up and hauling her into the pillows. She parted her legs for me, making space in the cradle of her hips.

I kissed her, letting her taste herself on my tongue. I kissed her until she was writhing again, begging for more.

In one long stroke, I thrust inside her tight body. One

long stroke, her walls fluttering around my length, and I nearly came undone.

"Fuck, Stell." It took every fiber of my strength not to come, feeling her heat as she stretched around me. I wrapped her in my arms, burying my face in her hair. "You feel so good."

She wrapped her arms around me, holding me close. "Move."

I kissed her pulse, then leaned away, pulling out to slam inside.

"Heath," she cried, her eyes squeezing shut.

I heard my name three more times from her lips before she came again, pulsing and squeezing me with such force that her orgasm triggered my own. I came on a roar, pulsing inside her as white stars broke behind my eyes.

Boneless and sated, I collapsed onto her arms, rolling so she was draped across my chest. Then I held her tight, feeling her heart beat in an opposite rhythm to my own.

How had I gone this long without her? Why hadn't we been doing this all along? She'd ruined me for other women.

One night, and I was ruined.

This was reckless. She was an employee. She was Guy's sister.

But she was Stella.

My Stella.

She made a move to stand, but I held her tight.

"Stay."

She pushed the hair from her face and gave me a sleepy smile. "Okay."

———

"STELLA?" I called through the house, yawning as I squinted at the bright light streaming through the windows. "Stella."

Silence.

I padded to the front door, peering through a sidelight. There were fresh tire tracks in my driveway, ones that hadn't been left by last night's Uber.

No, they'd likely been from this morning. After Stella had snuck out of the house.

"Damn it."

Why would she leave? Why wouldn't she wake me first? Was she upset?

I rubbed the stubble on my jaw, pissed at myself for not waking up and frustrated with her for sneaking out.

Any normal day, I'd track her down. I'd show up at her doorstep and we'd talk this through. But it wasn't a normal day.

It was Christmas.

Merry Christmas, Stella.

CHAPTER SEVEN

STELLA

op. Pop. Pop.
    As the popcorn cooked in my microwave, I tapped my finger to its sound while I stared unblinking at my kitchen cabinets.

I should call him. Should I call him? *Yes. Tomorrow. Maybe.*

The microwave beeped and I took out the bag, shaking it before dumping the white kernels in a glass bowl and retreating to my living room. I plopped onto the couch, shoved a handful of popcorn in my mouth and stared at the blank TV.

I'd been doing a lot of staring since sneaking out of Heath's bed on Christmas morning.

Mom had asked me fifteen times yesterday if I'd been feeling okay. I'd lied, promising that I'd been fine. But no, I was not okay. I was a flipping mess.

Heath had literally scrambled my brain. Any time I tried to think of any other subject—work, gifts, food—I'd get about two seconds down one train of thought only to be yanked back to his bed. I'd picture his broad shoulders pushing my knees apart as he'd licked me into oblivion.

A shiver raced down my spine.

Oral Sex Fan Club, meet your newest member, Stella Marten.

I'd had sex, lots of incredible sex with lots of incredible orgasms, with Heath Holiday. *My* Heath Holiday.

What did this mean? Did he want a relationship? Were coworkers allowed to be couples at Holiday Homes? Why now?

All questions I could have asked had I stuck around his house yesterday morning, but when I'd woken up deliciously sore, panic had taken over, so I'd slid out from beneath his arm and bolted.

Because this was Heath.

Heath.

How long had I dreamed of this? Of him? I'd fantasized about him for so long, I hadn't been prepared for this to ever become a reality. He'd exceeded every expectation, every dream. And in just one night.

It shouldn't have been so good, right? That was crazy. Wasn't it?

Maybe my juvenile delusions from years past were clouding reality. Maybe my teenage crush was bubbling to the surface. Maybe my subconscious was playing tricks on me because he was forbidden.

And terrifying.

One night and I'd screwed everything up. Because now I wanted him more than ever. And if he decided we'd been a mistake, well . . .

"I'll quit." That wasn't the worst thing in the world, right? I'd only been working at Holiday Homes since the beginning of the month. Maybe my old company would take me back if I begged. And took a pay cut.

Or . . . I could move. If Heath dumped me, I could move.

Yes, I would definitely have to move. I'd have to find a new town. A new job. A new house and a new guy.

If Heath didn't want me, there was no other choice.

"Yep. I'll move." I fisted another handful of popcorn, chewing with fury as anxiety raced through my veins.

I was going to have to move and change my entire life because Heath had ruined me.

Another handful went to my mouth, my cheeks bulging like a chipmunk, and I just kept shoving more in as I endured the hundredth mental freak-out in the past thirty-six hours.

Pull it together, Stella.

More popcorn was stuffed into my mouth. Wendy would be proud because usually, my stress eating involved McDonald's, a can of Reddi-wip and a family-sized bag of Funyuns. This popcorn wasn't even buttered.

Any other man and I'd throw myself into work as a distraction. But work meant Heath and luckily, the office was closed until after New Year's so I wouldn't have to face him quite yet.

"I don't want to move." I groaned, ready to toss the popcorn, find my keys and head to the nearest drive-thru when the doorbell rang.

With the bowl tucked in my arm, I shoved another bite into my mouth and went to answer, expecting Wendy or Guy since they were the only two people besides my parents who visited. It was after dark so Mom and Dad would already be glued to the History Channel.

I checked the peephole, finding Guy on the other side. His back was to me because he was looking at something on the street. I unlocked the door, swinging it open, just as he turned.

Not Guy.

Heath.

The popcorn in my mouth came shooting out in a stream of white confetti.

A soggy kernel landed on Heath's gray sweatshirt.

My eyes bulged as I watched him flick it off.

"Hi," he said.

I blinked.

He was wearing a Holiday Homes hoodie and a navy ballcap. Nearly the same navy Montana State ballcap my brother wore all the time. From the back, those hats were identical. But the fronts had different logos.

He'd duped me into opening the door. I should have looked closer at the hair color.

"May I come in?"

I blinked again.

Heath chuckled and stepped close, using his thumb to brush a popcorn piece off my chin.

"I just spit food on you," I whispered, my cheeks flaming.

Other people didn't get this version of me, the one intent on humiliating herself. Why did she only come out when Heath was around?

He lifted a shoulder, reached in to take a handful of popcorn, then came inside, shuffling me backward so he could close the door as he popped a few pieces into his mouth. His chiseled jaw flexed as he chewed.

No man had ever made popcorn so attractive. If he ever asked me on a movie date, I'd probably orgasm in the theater just by watching him eat popcorn.

He swallowed, his Adam's apple bobbing, then stomped his Nikes, clearing off the snow on the rug in my entryway. He took off his hat, only to turn it backward.

Holy. Shit. Why was that so hot? He was the older, rugged version of the boy I'd loved from afar. A man so utterly attractive I forgot to breathe. As I stood there drooling, his gaze raked up and down my body.

"Jesus, Stell. Are those your pajamas?"

I nodded.

He closed his eyes for a moment, his hands fisting like he was praying for restraint.

I glanced at my attire. The set was black satin, the pants wide and drapey. The top was basically a bra, showing my midriff beneath the jacket that went over the top that I hadn't bothered buttoning. "Sorry?"

He opened his eyes and closed the gap between us, fitting his palm against my cheek. "You ran out on me."

"I'm sort of freaking out. Like, a lot of freaking out." My free hand dove automatically into the bowl, but before I could scoop a handful for my mouth, Heath stole the popcorn and set it aside on the console table.

"Why are you freaking out?"

"Because now I have to move."

His eyebrows came together. "What? You're moving?"

I nodded. "I have to."

"Why?"

"Because we had sex. A lot of sex."

"We did? When?"

"Stop." I smacked his arm, relaxing as he laughed, and led him to the living room couch. I plopped down on one end as he took the other.

He looked so at ease, so confident, as he laid an arm over the back and crossed an ankle over his knee. "Be real with me. Are you okay?"

I melted a little at the worry in his voice and concern in those blue eyes. "Yes. Just . . . confused."

"Is that why you snuck out?"

"I don't do well when things are up in the clouds."

"In the clouds. What do you mean?"

"That saying. Up in the air. I say *up in the clouds* because clouds are fluffier, so if I'm going to be in limbo, I might as well be in the fluff."

He studied me, the corner of his mouth turning up. "That shouldn't make sense. But I guess it does."

"Did you have a nice Christmas?"

"I did. We just hung out at Mom and Dad's. Opened gifts. It was more exciting than normal years with Violet there."

"You're warming up to her."

"She's a terror and she'll turn Maddox gray before he hits forty, but yeah. She's a cool kid. I just came from Mom and Dad's. Mom declared a game night. Natalie was there too."

"Really?"

He grinned. "Maddox is crushing on her. Hard."

I loved that for my friend. Natalie deserved a sweet, billionaire hottie.

Maddox had graduated by the time I'd started high school, but his legend had lived on through the girls on the swim team. He'd been a lot like Heath. Handsome. Athletic. Popular. He'd become extremely wealthy since leaving Montana, but given the way Heath seemed to admire his older brother, I suspected Maddox had always kept his small-town roots.

"How was your Christmas?" he asked.

"Uneventful."

"Did Santa bring you anything good?"

"These pajamas."

"Well done, Santa."

My breath caught in my throat as his gaze raked down my chest and the shift in his expression. Heath looked like he was about to pounce, to drag me across the couch and have his way with me.

I would gladly be dragged.

But then he shook his head, shifting to dig something out of his jeans pocket. "I picked up something for you."

"Oh. You didn't need to get me anything."

"I know." He handed over a rectangular, black velvet case. "But I wanted to."

I sat up straighter, taking the box and flipping it open. Inside was a dainty gold bracelet with three jingling bells. The jewelry brought a smile to my lips. "This is beautiful. I used to have one just like it."

"I remember."

"You do? No way. That was ages ago."

"Your grandpa bought it for you, right?"

"Yes. He used to tease me that I walked silently and could be a ninja when I grew up." Grandpa had been a lot like Guy—loud in every way. So loud that he wouldn't hear me walk up. I'd startled him countless times, and each time, he'd let out this huge yelp before slapping a hand to his heart. "That bracelet was the last Christmas present he bought me."

"I was there the day it broke," he said. "You caught it on the swing set in your backyard, and you cried so hard I thought you were hurt."

I'd been devastated. And he'd remembered. He'd bought me a new one. My eyes flooded as I touched the bracelet. "Will you help me put it on?"

"Sure." He slid to the middle cushion, taking the jewelry from the box. Then he fastened it on my left wrist, his fingers warm against my skin.

I jingled it, smiling at the delicate chime. "Thank you."

"You're welcome." Heath's gaze was waiting when I looked up, and because I hadn't gotten him a gift, I rose up, pressing my lips to his.

It was meant to be a quick kiss, but one brush of our mouths and the heat between us ignited.

His arms wrapped me tight before he pressed me deeper into the toss pillows. His tongue swept between my teeth, stroking my own.

We kissed frantically, neither of us getting enough. Then the clothes between us began to disappear, item by item. His hoodie. My pants. His T-shirt. My top.

He settled between my thighs, his arousal hard and thick and long as it pressed into my throbbing core. "God, Stell."

"I can't believe this is happening," I whispered.

He positioned at my entrance, slowly, inch by inch, thrusting inside. "Believe it now?"

I shook my head, savoring the stretch of my body to fit his. "No."

"You will. Give it time."

Time with him was just another fantasy.

But before I could get stuck in my head, I was lost to Heath's body. I succumbed to the ragged breaths. To the rough touches. To the rhythm of his strokes and the thunder of my heart.

We came together, both crying out, as the orgasm stole my sight, blinding me to anything but this man.

My new bracelet jingled as I shoved the hair out of my eyes, coming down from the high. "Wow."

"Fuck, you are incredible." Heath twisted us so he was beneath me on the couch, our bodies slick with sweat. Then he stared at the ceiling. "I wasn't going to do this."

"Do what?"

He let a hand trail down my spine to cup my ass. "You."

I smiled. "Why not?"

"Because I want more than sex from you. But those goddamn pajamas from Santa were irresistible. They look even better on the floor."

I laughed, closing my eyes to memorize every second. His spicy scent. His hard body. The weight of his hand. The caress of his touch. The sound of his words still ringing in my mind.

Because I want more than sex from you.

There was a giddy laugh in my chest. The moment he

was gone, I was going to let it loose to bounce off the apartment walls.

"I can't stay."

"Oh." The disappointment in my voice filled my living room.

"I want to." He kissed my forehead. "But I'd better get going. Tobias was acting strange at Christmas yesterday, so I want to see if I can find out what's going on."

"Okay."

The two of us dressed and then walked to the door. When was he coming back? What would it be like at work? Should we tell Guy? The only men I'd ever slept with—all three of them—had been boyfriends before lovers. I was a woman who loved labels.

I opened my mouth to ask when I'd see him again, but I caught myself and faked a yawn. There was time to figure this out, right? We didn't have to answer all the questions tonight.

"Tired?" he asked.

I nodded. "Yeah. I'm going to hit the straw."

"Hit the hay."

"They don't put hay in stalls for the animals to sleep on. Did you know that? I went to a petting zoo once and asked the owner, and she told me they put straw in the pens and feed them hay. So you hit the straw."

"That's . . ." Heath's broad chest shook as he laughed. "Okay. Hit the straw."

"Thanks again for my bracelet." I twirled my wrist, loving the tiny jingle.

"Welcome." He inched closer, taking my face in his hands. "You're something special, Stella Marten."

And he was a dream.

With one last kiss goodbye, he winked and headed into the winter night. The smile on my face pinched my cheeks as I closed the door behind him.

Wendy. I had to call Wendy.

I hurried to the living room where I'd left my phone earlier, pulling up her name. But before I could call, the doorbell rang again. I skipped down the hall, my toes dancing that Heath had come back. "Hey th—"

Not Heath.

Guy.

"It's cold." He shuddered and stepped inside.

I peered past him, searching for Heath's truck. His taillights were at the edge of the parking lot.

"Are you going to close the door?" Guy asked, shrugging off his coat. He must not have seen Heath's truck in the dark because he would have asked an entirely different question.

"Oh, um . . . yeah." I stepped out of the way to shut away the chill. "What are you doing here?"

"I was bored. Thought I'd come over." He looked me up and down, his face souring. "Are those the pajamas Mom bought you?"

"Yes. What's wrong with them?"

"Aren't you supposed to button the top?"

I rolled my eyes and buttoned the outer shell. "Happy now?"

"I'll be happy if you have a beer."

All I had was wine and a bottle of vodka in the fridge. I'd never much enjoyed the taste of beer. "You came to the wrong house if you wanted beer."

"True." He walked toward the living room and my stomach dropped.

Oh, shit. Would he be able to smell the sex? Or Heath's cologne? *Please don't let there be a wet spot on my couch.*

Guy tipped his nose to the air. "Popcorn?"

I swiped up the bowl that Heath had set aside and carried it to Guy, shoving it toward his face, hoping all he'd smell was the salt. "Here."

"Thanks." He popped a kernel into his mouth. "No butter?"

"I can make a new batch with butter."

"Yes, please. Want to watch a movie?"

"No. Let's sit in the kitchen." I wouldn't be able to stop thinking about Heath if we sat on the couch and my brother would notice if I kept smiling like a fool.

"Why?"

"I was going to make some cookies," I lied.

"Not as good as beer, but I'll eat a cookie." Guy moved to the counter and took a seat on one of the barstools.

I rifled through my pantry, praying I had all of the

ingredients. I was out of flour, but I spied a box of brownie mix. "Oh, how about brownies instead? That actually sounds better."

"Fine by me." He shrugged, finishing the bowl of my popcorn. "So what did you do tonight?"

Your best friend.

I pulled in my lips to hide my smile as I gave him my back to retrieve a mixing bowl from the cupboard.

At some point, Heath and I would have to tell Guy. If this was more than sex. But considering I still wasn't sure exactly what our relationship would be like, there was no point telling my brother I'd slept with his best friend.

Twice.

CHAPTER EIGHT

HEATH

S tella's smile as she answered the door made my drive across town on icy roads worth every white-knuckled second. "Hi."

"Hi." I grinned and stepped inside, sweeping her into my arms and dipping her low for a kiss.

She smiled against my mouth, her hands instantly wrapping around my shoulders. When I finally stood her up, she laughed, the light in those hazel eyes dancing. "Trying to sweep me off my feet?"

"Maybe." I chuckled. "Is it working?"

"Yes."

"Good." I kissed her forehead, then kicked off my shoes before following her into the living room and joining her on the couch. "How was your day?"

"Busy. I deep cleaned, did laundry and braved Costco. You?"

"Worked for a while. Let Mom drag me downtown for shopping." I pulled a red square jewelry box out of my jeans pocket and handed it over. "For you."

"Another gift? That's two days in a row." She took the box. "Now I feel like I should have bought you a jumbo-sized box of Cheerios from the store."

"I do love my Cheerios."

"I know." She smiled. "Mom would always make sure to have them whenever you and Guy had sleepovers."

Looking back at our memories together was an unexpected thrill about being with Stella. It was fun to see what details she remembered. The ones I did.

Our history was the reason I'd had a near-constant smile since last night. It was like a piece had clicked into place. A piece I hadn't realized was missing.

Stella filled the gap.

She opened the box and another breathtaking smile stretched across her mouth. "Bows."

"I saw them and had to get them. They made me think of you."

"You thought of me?"

"Nonstop."

She blushed and pulled one of the earrings out of the box, a tiny golden bow adorned with rainbow-colored jewels. Stella put it in her ear, then did the same with the other. "I love rainbow colors."

"I know."

No sooner than the words had left my mouth, she

launched herself at me, flattening my back to the couch as she surged. I wrapped her tight, not wasting a second.

As much fun as it had been having sex on the couch, tonight, I wanted some space. So with her still in my arms, our mouths fused, I stood and carried her down the hallway, hoping like hell I found a bed.

My guess was solid.

We emerged from her room an hour later after a couple of orgasms and a shower.

Stella and I returned to the couch, and as I lay down, I tucked her into my side. A natural fit.

How many movies had we watched in the basement of her parents' house? How many nights had I missed doing this? Hell, I wouldn't have realized it even if I'd tried back then. As a teenaged boy, I hadn't been into cuddling with girls. I probably would have broken her heart, and then Guy would have had a good reason to kick my ass.

There was a reason he'd forbidden any of his friends from going near Stella. We'd all been as bad as him, looking for a score and nothing more. Except I'd grown out of that. The closer I got to thirty, the more casual hookups had lost their appeal. My last girlfriend had been months ago. But I liked commitment. I liked being tied to a person.

I wouldn't miss a chance at being tied to Stella.

"I like your place," I told her.

Her apartment was finished in neutrals, like most complexes around town. Beige walls. Taupe carpet. But she'd added pops of color with the furniture, decor and artwork. The TV stand was a bold coral. The toss pillow behind my head was teal. The coffee table was mustard yellow and the rug beneath had flecks of everything, pulling it all together.

Rainbow colors for my bright, beautiful girl.

"Thanks. It's just an apartment." She shrugged. "It's boring. But I'm saving to buy a house. I want a hefty down payment so it's taking me a while."

"Ever think about building? I know a guy who owns a construction company."

She smiled and curled deeper into my side. "Maybe, I, um . . . never mind."

"What?"

"Don't flip out, okay?"

"When a woman tells a man not to flip out, it means he's probably going to flip out."

"Fine." She zipped her lips shut.

I waited, listening to the clock tick on the wall. But the curiosity got the better of me as the second hand lapped the twelve twice. "Okay, fine. No flip-outs. Promise. Tell me what you were going to say."

"I want to get a house in a good school district. I know that marriage and kids are a ways off, and I'm not saying this about you, but it's a consideration because—"

"You're a planner."

"Exactly."

"I'm a planner too, Stell. Why do you think I bought the best lot in the best neighborhood with the best elementary school and built a five-bedroom house with a huge yard?" I wasn't going to live in that house by myself for the rest of my life.

"You're not freaked out by this?"

I shifted so I could get a better look at her face. "Ten years ago? Yeah. I would have been out the door. But I'm not here for a hookup or something casual."

She smiled but there was a wariness in her gaze.

Stella still didn't believe me. But she would.

I was all about exploring this thing with her. I wanted the first dates. I wanted the sleepovers. I wanted the calls when she was at the grocery store to see if I needed anything.

"I guess I'm still expecting you to react like Guy." She dropped her forehead to my chest, her beautiful blond hair draping around us.

"Guy's my best friend." I twisted a lock of her sunshine strands between my fingers. "But we're not the same. We're exploring this. Got it?"

"Got it," she breathed. "Thank you for my earrings."

"You're welcome."

She propped her chin up on her hands. "How was Tobias?"

"I don't know. He wasn't home and he didn't answer when I called." Ten times. I'd left here last night to track him down but wherever he'd been, he hadn't wanted to be found.

"Guy showed up after you left."

Then it was probably a good thing I'd been gone. Having him show up and see us together would not be a good way to tell him I was claiming his sister. "I'll talk to him."

"Maybe I should."

"No, it should be me." If I was in his shoes, I'd want my friend to tell me. I wouldn't put this on Stella.

"Okay." She sighed. "How do you think he'll take it?"

"I don't know," I lied.

Guy was going to rage. He'd probably try and pick a fight. But she was worth a few punches. If that's what it took, I'd let Guy hit me square in the face.

We lay together, just breathing, until she yawned.

"I should let you hit the straw."

She laughed. "Do you want to stay?"

"Yes, but I'd better get home. I am going to swing by Tobias's place again. See if I can catch him."

"Okay." She shifted, standing from the couch. "When . . . never mind."

"Say it."

"When will I see you again?"

I ran my fingers over her cheek. "Was that so hard to ask?"

"I don't want you to think I'm clingy."

"But you are clingy."

She frowned and a cute little crease formed between her eyebrows. "No, I'm not."

"It's not an insult, baby. I know you. Like you know

me. I like that you want to plan when we'll see each other again. I like that you're trying to be chill about this, but Stella, I'm not chill about this. So you don't need to be either."

Never in my life had I thought about a woman as much as I'd thought about Stella since the party. Never had I watched the clock, waiting for the right time to go over. Never had I planned to see a woman day after day after day.

"This is happening so fast." She shook her head. "I'm still catching up."

"You will." I kissed her again. "Get some rest. Tomorrow night I'm staying and there won't be much sleep."

Her face lit up. "Promise? Maybe I should hydrate."

I chuckled. "Definitely hydrate. And make no plans for Thursday morning."

If we were both on vacation, we might as well enjoy it.

With another kiss at the door, I left her for the frigid winter air. I slid behind the wheel of my truck, cranked the heat, intending to hunt down my brother and find out what had crawled up his ass this week. But as I pulled onto the street, I made a last-second decision to search for another brother instead.

The drive to Guy's condo was short. He'd bought a place close to Stella's apartment on purpose, saying he wanted to be around in case she needed help. In reality, it was because he was just as clingy as Stella and craved attention. So on the nights when there wasn't anything else to entertain him, he'd visit his sister.

Their parents still lived in the neighborhood where I'd grown up. That was before both Mom's and Dad's businesses had boomed and they'd decided to build a massive home in the mountain foothills.

My parents, also planners, had added plenty of bedrooms for future grandchildren.

I parked next to Guy's truck and went straight for the door, squaring my shoulders as I rang the bell. There was no time to overthink this. He was going to be pissed so I might as well get it over with.

"Hey." He swung the door open, lifting the beer bottle in his hand. "Good timing. I just opened this. Want one?"

"Sure." I stepped inside. "But do you have any cans?"

He gave me a strange look. "Uh . . . yeah."

"Then I'll have a can."

That bottle was a weapon. I'd wait to tell him about Stella until he'd finished drinking and it was safely stowed in the garbage where it couldn't be broken in half over my skull.

Guy led the way to his fridge, pulling out a Bud Light.

"Thanks." I popped the top and gulped.

"What are you doing tonight?" he asked. "Maybe after we finish these we could head downtown."

"Maybe." I walked to the living room off the kitchen, sitting down in a chair that faced the TV. My knee began bouncing.

Guy sank into his couch and grabbed the remote to mute EPSN. "Can I ask you something?"

Shit. He knew. The fucker already knew. "What's up?"

"Have any guys been visiting Stella at work?"

"Uh, no." I gave him a sideways glance, keeping an eye on that beer bottle. It would hurt like a motherfucker if he threw it at my face. "Why?"

"I think she's dating someone."

I blinked. Was this a trick?

"So?" He raised his eyebrows.

I took a gulp of my beer to clear my throat. "So, what?"

"So have you seen anyone come to work? Take her out to lunch or anything?"

"No."

He frowned. "Huh."

I waited for more. I waited for an attack. But he simply sat there, pondering my answer. "Why do you think she's dating?"

"I went over to her place last night. She was wearing this slutty pajama outfit thing and when she opened the door, it was like she expected me to be someone else."

Me. She'd expected him to be me.

This was the perfect opportunity to spill and get it over with. But did I fess up? Did I tell him that those pajamas weren't slutty and that if he ever used the word *slut* in the same sentence as his sister's name again I'd break his nose? No. I sat there like a coward.

"So what if she's seeing someone?" I took another long drink. "She's an adult."

"I don't like that she's hiding it from me."

Tell him. "Maybe it's new and she doesn't want to introduce the guy to her family yet."

He shook his head. "She should still tell me. After the shit she went through in college, she knows I worry."

"Wait. What?" I set my beer down and leaned forward. "What shit in college?"

He took a drink, draining his bottle dry. "You can't tell her I told you. She made me promise not to tell."

"Of course. What happened?"

"This friend of mine. Former friend. He lived in our dorm freshman year."

"Which friend?"

"Dave."

Dave. I searched my memory, trying to place a Dave with a face. Who the fuck was Dave? The name was growing more familiar, but I couldn't put it with a face. "Did I know him?"

Guy shook his head. "No. He lived on the fourth floor. I'd go up and play video games with him sometimes."

Video games hadn't ever been my thing and I'd spent my freshman year in class while Guy had barely passed. He'd aced the art of skipping. The days when I'd been taking notes in a lecture hall, he'd been with *Dave.*

"How would Stella know him?" She hadn't come to

MSU until long after we'd left the dorms for our apartment off campus.

"I kept in touch with him." Guy's jaw clenched. "We had a couple of core classes together. I'd meet him in the library to study. One day, Stella was there with me. I introduced them. And . . ."

"And?"

His nostrils flared. "He took her out. Didn't tell me about it. She went with him to a frat party, and he slipped something into her drink."

My temperature spiked from normal to boiling in a flash. I was seconds from exploding as my arms began to shake and my hands balled so tight my nails dug into my palms. I didn't trust myself to speak so I sat there, my jaw locked, and waited for him to continue.

"I showed up at the party too. Thank fuck. Showed up right as he was trying to drag her off to a room. She was totally out of it. I've never seen her like that. It scared the hell out of me."

"Tell me you beat the shit out of Dave."

"I beat the shit out of Dave. That's the reason I got banned from every frat house."

Guy had told me about the fight, just not the reason it had started. I'd rolled my eyes at the time because, by our junior year, I'd been more focused on school than I had been on partying. But not Guy.

Now I wish I would have been with him. Now I wish I would have met Dave.

"After that, I made Stella promise to tell me when she started dating anyone," he said.

"Why didn't I know about this?"

"Like I said, she made me promise. It shook her up. She was really embarrassed, and it was hard for her to trust anyone for a while."

For that alone, I wanted to strangle Dave. I dragged a hand through my hair. "I had no idea."

"No one does. She didn't even tell Mom and she tells Mom just about everything."

Damn. This was certainly not what I'd expected to hear coming over tonight.

"I just . . ." He smacked a hand on his leg. "I have a feeling she's seeing someone."

Yeah. Me. "Her freshman year was a long time ago."

"She's my sister, man. I don't want anything to happen to her."

"Maybe the guy she's seeing isn't a Dave. Maybe he's decent."

Guy scoffed. "Or maybe he's a prick."

"Come on." My heart was racing again. The conversation hadn't gone as I'd expected so far, but maybe that would work in my favor. Compared to the fuckwad Dave, I was a saint, right? I would never disrespect Stella, Guy had to know that. "What if she was dating someone like me?"

Or me.

Guy started laughing. "That's my nightmare, man. That's my nightmare."

"What? Why?"

"Dude. You slept with half the cheerleaders our senior year."

"In high school. That was over ten years ago. And you slept with the other half."

"Exactly. The last person I want Stella with is anyone like you and me. She's too good."

I couldn't exactly argue with that. Stella was as pure and perfect as they came. But damn it, I wanted to earn her. I liked to think so far, I was doing a good job.

Guy stood, picking up his beer bottle. He took a step like he was going to head to the kitchen for another, but stopped and glanced over his shoulder. "This is all rhetorical, right? You're joking."

"Uh, yeah." *Heath, you spineless bastard.*

"Good. Because I'd have to kill you if you ever went after my sister."

I tipped the beer can to my lips, using it to hide my disappointment as he left the room.

Guy wanted a decent man for Stella.

Apparently, he didn't think his best friend fit that bill.

Fucking hell. How could he not think I was good enough? I had a great job. A fantastic house. So what if I hadn't dated much? I hadn't met a woman who made me want a long-term commitment. Until Stella.

I shoved out of my seat, taking my beer can to the

kitchen. I dumped out the dregs and put the can in the recycling bin beneath the sink. Because decent men recycled and I was a fucking decent man.

"I'm going to take off."

"What?" Guy popped out of the fridge, two fresh beers in his hand. "You just got here."

"I remembered something I needed to do for work," I lied.

"I thought you guys were closed this week."

"Just because the office is closed doesn't mean I don't have work to do."

"Fine," he muttered with a scowl. "You're in a piss mood anyway."

Nice. "Bye." Without another word, I walked to the door, ripped it open with too much force and marched to my truck. The blood roaring in my veins kept me warm as I drove to Stella's apartment and stood at her door, waiting for her to answer.

The deadbolt flipped first, then there she was. Tonight's pajamas were a tie-dyed sleepshirt that hit her at the knees. The arms were so big they draped to her elbows. "Hi."

"Hi." I stepped inside. "So I just left Guy's place."

"W-what?"

"I went over to tell him that I was going to ask you on a date."

"You did?"

I nodded and fisted my hands on my hips. "Yep. It went great," I deadpanned.

Stella cringed. "Is he mad?"

"No, I didn't tell him." But he'd told me plenty.

Plenty that I couldn't bring up, not yet. Someday soon, I wanted to hear Stella's side of the story with Dave. But I was too angry about it tonight. When—if—she wanted to talk, I needed to be there to listen, not fume.

"He was in a shit mood," I lied. "Thought it would be better to wait. You know how he is."

"Yes, I do." Her shoulders fell and she tugged at the collar of her shirt. "What now?"

We didn't have a lot of options. Not until I told Guy.

So I tucked a lock of hair behind her ear. "Can you keep a secret?"

CHAPTER NINE

STELLA

Two days wasn't exactly a long time to keep a secret. Okay, it was nothing. Two days was nothing.

But I really, *really* hated keeping secrets.

After Heath had asked me if I could keep a secret, of course I'd lied and said yes. I mean . . . what was my other option? Kick him out? Deny him sex? Absolutely not.

This secret might be torturing me, but I'd endure it for the orgasms alone.

Last night, Heath had stayed over, exhausting me with his fingers and tongue and cock. But tonight, we were switching beds, and he was cooking me dinner at his house.

I hurried around my bedroom, rushing to pack a bag. It rested on the foot of my bed, overflowing. So far I'd grabbed a change of clothes for tomorrow. A plum, sheer negligee I'd splurged on this afternoon at the mall. My toiletries were stuffed in a travel case along with my hair dryer because my hair wasn't the type that air-dried well. Then there was my makeup and brushes.

I stared at the bag and the curling wand in my hand, debating adding it to the mix.

Or I could get a suitcase. In my suitcase, it would all fit, no problem. I wanted to be comfortable. But Heath had been a saint so far, not getting spooked by my talk of the future. If I showed up with a suitcase, it might be the final straw.

This was the type of dilemma I'd normally run by Wendy. She'd called me four times in the past two days, trying to catch up. I'd avoided her at every call. Because the minute I spoke to her, I'd spill. So calling my best friend wasn't an option.

The suitcase-versus-backpack quandary was one I'd have to solve myself.

I'd avoided Guy just as deliberately as I had Wendy. He'd showed up at lunch today. I'd hidden beneath a blanket on the couch and held my breath until he'd finally stopped ringing the doorbell and left.

I couldn't avoid them forever. We couldn't keep this a secret forever. Didn't Heath want to tell people? Because I was ready to shout it from rooftops.

Heath Holiday was having sex with me.

That sentence would sound great from the top of my lungs.

Heath was the greatest kisser in the world. How did I know this? Because he was kissing me.

Heath was an excellent snuggler. A fact I'd verified after he'd slept in my bed.

Heath. Was. Mine.

Mine.

God, I wanted to tell someone. Anyone. Then maybe I'd actually believe this was happening.

"I'm spending the night at Heath's house."

Saying it to my empty bedroom wasn't quite as therapeutic as I'd hoped. Oh, well. Keeping a secret for a few more days would give us a chance to feel this out. Heath and I could decide together when to bring friends and family into the mix.

A few more days, then we could tell Guy. When we were sure.

Except I hadn't asked Heath how long this would be a secret. He wouldn't want this to go on for too long, right? No way.

And if this didn't work, well . . . it would be best if Guy didn't know.

My stomach churned at the idea of a breakup.

I studied the curling wand again. While I had him, I was at least going to have good hair, so I tossed it into the pile, then worked to stuff everything into the backpack. I had to sit on it to get the zipper closed and it bulged at the seams.

It was dark beyond the windows as I shrugged on my

coat, the winter days short. I loaded up, my bag straining my shoulders, and rushed to my car.

The drive across town to Heath's house was slow, the clouds that had been hanging over town all day finally opening up to dump a fresh coat of snow, and my tires crunched on the quiet streets as I navigated Heath's neighborhoods.

This was one of the best areas in Bozeman. Heath had built his house on a large corner lot, giving himself some distance from the house next door. Three blocks from here was an elementary school.

I imagined kids wearing backpacks nearly as heavy as mine walking down these safe sidewalks, meeting up with their friends along the way. That's how it had been in my youth. Guy and I would leave our house first, stopping to collect Heath, Tobias and Maddox on the way to school. The boys would walk ahead, though sometimes, Heath would hang back and walk beside me instead.

All those years ago, from the time I'd been just a little girl, and I'd never stopped hoping he'd walk by my side.

I smiled as I parked, collected my bag and made my way to the door. Before I could knock, he was there, a sexy smile on that handsome face.

"Hi." He reached for my backpack, taking it from my arm. "I figured you would have brought a little suitcase."

My mouth parted. "How did you know?"

He chuckled and waved me inside. "Because you don't carry a purse. You carry a tote. I've never once seen you pack light. Remember that weekend when your parents were going out of town for their anniversary and you guys stayed with us? You brought three bags for one night."

"I don't know how to pack light."

"You don't have to pack light." He tucked a lock of hair behind my ear. "Not for me. Bring whatever you want. I'll haul it inside."

My heart skipped. I wasn't sure what to say so I rose up on my toes to brush my mouth against his, then stepped inside.

The house smelled like Heath, spicy and male and clean.

"Give me your keys." He held out his hand.

I placed them in his palm. "Why?"

"I'm going to park your car inside. Keep it out of the snow."

Or keep it secret? I shook that thought away, irritated at myself that I'd assume his kind gesture was to hide us. "Here you go."

"Be right back." He set my backpack aside, then walked for the door. "Make yourself at home."

"Okay." I waited until he was outside, then wandered into the house.

When I'd been here on Christmas Eve, I'd been too busy kissing Heath to look around. And the morning after, when I'd snuck out, I'd lingered by the door, watching for my Uber.

As expected, Heath's home was as classy as the man himself.

Rich wood pieces and buttery leather furniture filled the living room. Maple cabinets hugged the kitchen's walls, circling a black, granite island. The charcoal walls and coal rugs added to the moody, manly vibe.

I could live here. Definitely.

"Getting ahead of yourself again." I giggled, walking to the kitchen.

On the counter closest to the gas range rested a cutting board and knife along with a tomato and box of baby spinach.

The garage door hummed as it closed on the other end of the house, then Heath strode into the main room. He went straight for my backpack still by the front door, winking at me as he carted it down the hallway toward his bedroom.

When he returned, he walked right to me, taking my face in his hands to kiss me. "Hi."

"Hi."

"Thanks for coming over."

I smiled. "Thanks for dinner."

"Don't thank me yet. I'm not the best cook."

"Want some help?"

"No, you sit." He nodded to the barstools at the island. "Wine?"

"Sure."

Uncorking the bottle and pouring us each a glass was the only thing Heath didn't fumble with in the kitchen.

I bit the inside of my cheek to keep from laughing when he went to slice the tomato and half of it rolled to the floor. I stayed quiet when he read the instructions meticulously on the box of uncooked fettuccini noodles. But when he took out the chicken breasts from the fridge and realized they were still frozen, I couldn't help it anymore and slid off my seat.

"Shit." He shook his head. "I took these out this morning. Guess I should have done it last night. How do you feel about pizza delivery?"

"Or we can improvise." I joined him beside the cutting board, stealing the knife from his hand. "Do you have any mushrooms or broccoli?"

"Both, actually." He retrieved them from the fridge.

"Perfect. Put a pot of water on the stove to boil and add a bit of salt."

"Yes, ma'am." Heath gave me a mock salute, and after I rescued dinner, we returned to the island with bowls of creamy pasta primavera.

He forked a bite and moaned. "This is awesome."

I shrugged. "Mom's a great cook. I always liked helping her."

"You have her talent. This summer I'll wow you with my grilling skills."

"This summer?" Would we be together this summer?

He met my gaze, his locked with mine, and answered my unspoken question. "This summer."

I smiled through the meal and while I watched Heath do the dishes. Then we retreated to the living room, cuddling on the couch.

"Want to watch something?" he asked.

"Sure. You pick."

He reached for the remote, turning on the TV just as a flicker of headlights came through the front window.

We froze, listening for a long moment, but then he shot off the couch.

"Damn," he said, glancing out the windows.

"What?" I stood but didn't follow him toward the glass. "Is it Guy?"

"It's Tobias." He raked a hand through his hair.

"Oh."

He turned and gave me a pained look. "I've been trying to talk to him."

"You should. I can go."

"Would you mind just . . . hiding in the bedroom?"

My mouth parted. I had to hide? Of course, I had to hide. I was a secret. "Um, yeah. Okay."

I took a step to head that way, but Heath stopped me. "Don't forget your glass."

"Right." I picked it up from the end table because we couldn't have any evidence I was here. Good thing he'd already stowed my overnight bag.

"Sorry, Stell."

"It's fine," I lied with too much cheer. Then before he could see my face fall, I hurried down the hallway and eased the bedroom door shut.

"Hey." Heath's voice carried from the front door as he opened it for Tobias. "What's going on? I've been calling you."

"Yeah." Tobias stomped his feet, then from the sound of their steps, walked to the kitchen. "Got any more of that wine?"

That was my wine he was drinking.

I frowned and slunk to the bed, sitting on the edge. The plush comforter was the same shade of gray as the walls in the living space. The pillows were fluffed against the headboard made from narrow slats of wood, each stained in different colors like a small-scale version of barnwood.

Another beautiful, masculine room. Though it needed color. The whole house could use more color.

God, I felt like a fool. Sitting in here alone, thinking some ruby-red toss pillows would add some charm to Heath's room.

This secret thing was supposed to be for Guy. Why did we need to hide from Tobias? Why not just tell him we were together? Unless Heath was worried that Tobias would slip. Guy and Tobias weren't as close as Heath and my brother, but they were all friends. Or maybe it was a work thing. Maybe it was frowned upon for intra-office relationships.

Probably something I should have asked Heath before sleeping with him. *Sorry, not sorry.*

"Okay, what's going on?" Heath asked Tobias.

It was impossible not to eavesdrop. But if Heath didn't want me to listen, he should have sent me to the garage for an escape. There was nothing to do but sip my wine as their voices carried my way.

"You remember Eva?" Tobias asked Heath.

"Yeah."

There was a long pause. "She's pregnant."

I sat up straight.

Heath choked, coughing to clear his throat. "What?"

"She's pregnant. We hooked up a few months ago. I guess the condom broke because she showed up on Christmas Eve to tell me she was pregnant."

"That's why you weren't at the party."

"Yeah," Tobias muttered.

So focused on Heath and my champagne, I hadn't realized Tobias had been missing from the party.

"So what now?" Heath asked. "Is she keeping the baby? Are you guys getting back together?"

"She's moving to London." Tobias's voice was thick like he struggled to speak the words. "She leaves on New Year's."

"Fuck," Heath hissed.

My hand came to my heart, rubbing at the ache. I knew Eva. We'd met in college when she and Tobias had been together. The few parties when Guy had invited me

along—I'd always gone in the hopes of seeing Heath—
she'd been there too.

Eva was gorgeous and smart. She was one of the most
driven women I'd ever met. The two of us had lost touch
after she and Tobias had broken up—I wasn't sure why
they'd called it quits because they'd always been great
together. But shortly after their graduation, I'd heard from
Guy that she'd moved away from Montana.

I guess at some point she'd come back.

And now she was having Tobias's baby. *Whoa.*

"I don't know what to do," Tobias confessed. "I just . . .
I can't even wrap my head around this."

"You will," Heath promised. "Give it time. Talk to her.
You guys will figure this out."

"I'll miss it. I'll miss it all because she'll be halfway
around the world."

"Go with her," Heath said.

Tobias scoffed. "My life is here. Mom. Dad. You. Hell,
even Maddox is moving home."

"We're your family no matter where you live, brother."

The affection in Heath's voice melted my heart. I
wasn't crazy about sitting here, feeling like I was intruding
on a personal conversation. But to hear Heath, it reminded
me of all the reasons why no one had ever measured up.

He loved his family. He loved his friends.

"What about work?" Tobias asked. "Dad's going to
retire before too long. Then it will be ours."

"There's no reason you have to live here to help run

the company. You're in your office most days as it is. We'll get Maddox to buy you your own plane as a baby shower gift. God knows he can afford it."

I smiled, hoping that Tobias had one on his face too.

"I don't want to leave Montana," Tobias said. "When I think about having a family, raising a kid. This is where that needs to happen. Eva . . . she travels everywhere. She doesn't even have a permanent address."

Another long pause and I knew where this conversation was going.

My heart twisted again.

If Tobias wanted to stay here, either he'd have to convince Eva to give up her life or . . .

He'd have to fight for their child. He'd have to fight to keep the baby here.

"She'll hate me." Tobias's voice was so quiet I strained to hear. "If I push to keep the baby here, she'll hate me. But I don't want my child living out of temporary homes. Being passed from nanny to nanny. I don't want to see my kid every other weekend and holiday."

"You need to talk to Eva." There was a clap, like Heath had put his hand on Tobias's shoulder. "I know you both will want the best for your kid. You'll figure it out."

"Yeah." Tobias blew out a long breath. "How about a refill?"

The cork plunked out of the bottle and I heard the unmistakable glug of a glass being poured.

"Want to watch a game or something?" Tobias asked.

"I'm not quite ready to head home. I need to think of what to say to Eva first."

"Oh, uh . . ." Heath hesitated. "Sure."

I groaned and brought my own glass to my lips, gulping the rest of my wine. As the TV volume turned on, I set the empty glass aside and flopped back on the bed, staring at the white ceiling.

This was dumb. I felt like an idiot hiding in Heath's room. But it was too late to come out now. What would I say?

Oh, hi, Tobias. Sorry to hear about Eva. Congrats on the baby.

Maybe we could have made an excuse for me being here when Tobias had arrived. A work question or something to do with Guy. But it was too late now, so my only choice was to hide here.

And wait.

Thirty minutes passed. Tobias stayed. Then an hour. Then two.

"Stella." A hand on my shoulder shook me awake.

I jolted up, forgetting for a moment where I was. I'd fallen asleep waiting for Tobias to leave. "Is he gone?"

"Yeah. Sorry."

I pushed up on an elbow, glancing at the clock on the nightstand. It was after midnight.

"He wanted to stay for a game. I don't know if you heard or not—"

"I did. Sorry. It was sort of hard not to listen."

"It's fine. Saves me from rehashing it all. Anyway . . . I didn't want to kick him out."

"I get it."

"So much for dinner and a movie, huh? I'm sorry. We should have just told him you were here."

"He probably needed to talk and wouldn't have if I was there." I gave him a sad smile. "Should I go?"

"No. Stay. Please."

"All right."

The guilt on his face eased my stinging pride. "I'm sorry."

"It's okay."

Except it didn't feel okay. Because he might be sorry, but I had this awful feeling that it wouldn't matter.

And that come tomorrow morning, I'd still be his secret.

CHAPTER TEN

HEATH

Twenty-nine years old and I'd never given a woman flowers. Not Mom—Dad had always had her covered. Not my prom dates—they hadn't wanted wrist corsages. Not a girlfriend—there hadn't been many.

I guess I'd simply been waiting for the right woman. With a bouquet of twelve red roses clutched in one hand, I held my breath and pressed Stella's doorbell.

She answered moments later wearing a pair of ripped jeans and a red turtleneck the same color as the flowers. Her hair was curled. Her makeup accentuated those pretty eyes and long, sooty lashes. And in her ears, she wore the earrings I'd bought this week.

"Hi." She smiled, lifting a hand to tuck a lock of hair behind her ear and the faint jingle sound confirmed she was also wearing my bracelet.

I'd be adding more gifts to her collection. The jewelry I'd bought simply because I'd thought of her, but seeing her wear it was a rush I hadn't expected. It was almost as thrilling as it had been to wake up to her in my bed this morning.

"Hi." I leaned in to kiss her cheek, then stepped inside and handed over the bouquet.

"Thank you." She pressed them to her nose, humming as she inhaled their fragrance. "These are beautiful."

"I'm hoping they'll buy me a date."

"A date?" She arched an eyebrow. "What kind of date?"

"The real kind. You. Me. A nice restaurant. Good wine."

"Is that, um . . . allowed?"

"Why not?" I shrugged.

Last night had been a train wreck. When Tobias had showed up, I'd panicked. Not just because he was Guy's friend too, but because I wanted to talk to Dad about Stella first. We didn't need awkward tension in the office. After New Year's, I'd sit him down and explain. Until then, we'd keep this quiet.

Having Stella hide in my room was not how I'd planned the night to go, especially leaving her alone for hours. But Tobias had clearly been avoiding his own home —he'd stayed longer than he had after my Super Bowl party last year.

Tonight, I'd make it up to her.

Dinner downtown was a risk, but Guy had texted me earlier inviting me to a poker game at another friend's house. Tobias was home. Maddox was home. My parents were home, soaking up time with Violet.

I'd called them all earlier just to make sure of everyone's plans.

And if we did bump into anyone we knew, we could just pretend it was a work dinner.

"Sounds fun." She smiled and motioned to her outfit. "Should I change?"

"No. You're gorgeous."

Her cheeks flushed as she smelled the roses again. "Let me put these in some water."

While she took care of the flowers and pulled on some shoes and her coat, I called Bozeman's newest steakhouse and made a last-minute reservation.

"Why am I nervous?" Stella asked as we left her apartment.

"Nerves? Or excitement?" Because the jitters I was feeling were from the latter.

"Both," she breathed, slipping her hand in mine.

I loved how she was honest with me. That she didn't keep her thoughts to herself.

Stella looked perfect in the passenger seat of my truck, her perfume filling the cab. As we walked from the parking space to the restaurant, her arm rested comfortably in mine, like this was how we should have always walked together. The hostess seated us at a table in the corner of the room, handing us our menus to read by the dim light.

"Want me to order for you?" Stella asked.

"Isn't it customary for the man to order for his date?" Not that I would. She could have whatever she wanted.

"You've been proving how well you know me this week. It's my turn to take a stab at it."

"All right." I closed my menu and set it aside.

She smiled, challenge accepted, and scanned the book. Then she set it aside and shot me a smirk as our waitress came over. Stella ordered wine first, a rich cabernet that I would have picked myself.

After bringing over the bottle and filling our glasses, the waitress took out her notepad. "And what are we having this evening?"

"I'm going to have your filet. Medium with a baked potato, please," Stella said, glancing my way. "And he's going to have the rib eye. Medium rare with fries."

I grinned as the waitress scribbled down her notes and left us to our wine.

"So?" Stella asked.

"Nailed it."

"Yes." She fist-pumped and lifted her wineglass to clink with mine.

I laughed, ready to take a sip when my eyes landed on a familiar face walking our way. My smile dropped. "Shit."

Dad crossed the restaurant with Mom on his arm.

"What?" Stella followed my gaze. "Oh."

So much for our date.

"Hey, you two." Dad extended a hand as I stood. "How's it going?"

"Good." I nodded, my mind racing.

As far as I knew, there had never been an office relationship at Holiday Homes. We didn't have an official policy against it, but tonight was not the night to discuss it with my father. Not until Stella and I'd had more time together. Not until we'd told Guy.

And just like last night with Tobias, I panicked.

"Stella and I were at the office." The lie spewed from my lips in a desperate attempt to make this not look exactly as it was. A date. "We were both hungry and I remembered you mentioning this place was good."

"Ah." Dad nodded. "It is good. I didn't realize you were both working today."

"Just catching up on emails," I lied again, hating the way Stella's spine stiffened.

"I was, um . . . running some new numbers for the Jensen remodel." Her eyes flickered to mine for the fastest glare in history.

"Joe cornered me at the party," Dad said. "Told me about the flooring. Sounds like you handled it just right."

"Thanks." Stella gave him a smile, then turned to Mom. "Hi, Mrs. Holiday."

"Hannah," Mom corrected. "Please. And we'll let you kids get back to dinner."

"Unless you'd like to join us?" The invitation came so fast I said it before I thought about the words.

Fuck. Me. What was wrong with me?

"Are you sure?" Mom asked, looking between the two of us.

"Why not?" I held out the chair on my other side for her as Dad took the fourth.

The hostess appeared, bringing with her the other two place settings she'd cleared away earlier. Then the waitress hurried over so we could order another bottle of wine before Mom and Dad placed their orders.

Stella sat rigidly, her hands clasped on her lap, and kept her attention on my parents.

Tell them. Just tell them. I opened my mouth but Dad spoke before I had the chance.

"How was your Christmas, Stella?" he asked her.

"It was lovely," she said. "I spent the day at my parents' house and relaxed. You?"

"We did the same. Let Violet entertain us." Dad chuckled. "That girl is going to give Maddox a run for his money when she hits sixteen."

"Good thing he's worth billions," I teased.

Mom laughed. "Isn't that the truth. Stella, how's Guy doing?"

At the mention of Guy, Stella seemed to throw up even more of a guard. On the surface, she wore her beautiful, enchanting smile, but it didn't reach her eyes. "He's good. Still working as a programmer."

"I never quite understood how he got into computers." Mom shook her head. "For a person who thrives around people, I always thought he'd become a teacher or a coach or a used car salesman."

"Can you imagine Guy teaching kids?" Stella groaned. "That's terrifying."

We all laughed because she wasn't wrong.

Tell them.

Every time I opened my mouth, either my mother or father would speak first. And as the minutes passed, as the conversation carried on, it became harder and harder to find an explanation for lying in the first place.

Damn it. When they walked up to the table, I should have just told them. Dad wouldn't care, right? I'd have to wait and find out at work next week. So I sipped my wine and ate my meal while Stella completely charmed my parents.

She gave them her fullest attention, answering their questions and listening to stories. It was me who was ignored. Through the conversation and our meal, her cold shoulder became as frigid as the winter temperatures.

It was only after our plates were cleared, the tab was paid—by Dad, insisting that he'd expense it since this had been a *staff* dinner—and we were all bundled in our coats, did Stella finally glance my direction.

Her expression was flat. Guarded.

God, I was an asshole.

"Where did you park, Stella?" Dad asked as we congregated on the sidewalk outside the restaurant. "It's dark so we'll walk you."

"I got it. We parked in the same lot," I lied. Again.

That was the tenth or maybe the twentieth lie tonight. I'd lost track. Dad had bought them all. Mom, not even a little bit. Probably because I was a shit liar and Mom had always had a nose for when her sons were being devious.

She looked between Stella and me, and if Mom's expression had a name, it would be *You're Not Fooling Me, Son.*

I'd seen it countless times in my life. Usually before she'd grounded me for doing something stupid. Like the time I'd hauled my sled onto the roof so I could *get some air* and instead of hitting the snowbank beneath the eaves, I'd crashed through the neighbor's fence.

"So lovely seeing you, Stella." Mom pulled her into a hug.

Dad shook Stella's hand. "Don't worry about the Jensen project. Enjoy the rest of your vacation. Same to you, Heath."

"Will do."

Dad held out his arm to escort Mom, and with a wave, they headed down the street.

I sighed when they disappeared around a corner. "I'm sorry."

"It's fine." Stella nodded and spun in the other direction, starting down the sidewalk toward where we'd parked.

It was definitely not fine. Her shoes made an angry click as we walked. She kept her hands stuffed into the pockets of her jacket, her shoulders bunched at her ears.

Any time I moved closer, she'd inch away or walk faster. And at the truck, when I moved to open her door, she waved me off for the driver's side.

The trip to her apartment was silent, the tension growing thicker with every turn. When I parked in front of her place, she bolted out the door before I'd even put the truck in park.

"Damn it," I muttered. Then I was rushing after her, jogging to catch up before she could shut me out. "Stella, I'm sorry."

"It's fine." She fit her key into the lock. "We're a *secret.*"

The last word was so enunciated that I felt every letter like the whack of a hammer against a nail's head. *S-E-C-R-E-T*.

"I need to tell Dad. Make sure he's okay with it. I should have just done it tonight but . . . I'm sorry."

Stella looked up over her shoulder. "And if he's not okay with it?"

"He will be." He would be. He had to be. There wasn't another choice. "There's a chance that he'll ask us to be discreet."

She dropped her gaze, her shoulders falling. "More secrets?"

"It's not forever." I put my hands on her shoulders as I leaned in closer. "I panicked tonight. I didn't think we'd see anyone."

One minute she was starting to lean into my touch, the next she was shoving the door open and storming inside. *Shit.* Maybe I shouldn't talk tonight. I hadn't said a damn thing right.

I stayed on the stoop, watching as she stripped off her coat and hung it up on a hook. "Stell. I want to tell people. I want to tell Guy first."

"Then tell him." She tossed up her hands, standing close to the threshold like a blockade. "I don't like being a secret. I don't like lying to people, especially my brother, my boss and my boss's wife."

"You're right." I held up my hands. "I'm sorry."

She dropped her chin, staring at the floor for a long moment. Then she looked up and the shame in her eyes made me feel about three inches tall. "I know it's only been a week. Less than a week. But you're . . . you. I want to tell people about you. Because I like you. I like you a lot."

"I like you too. More than a lot. I'll tell them. My Dad. Mom. Guy. Tobias. I'll tell them all."

She blew out a long breath. "When?"

"Next week. First thing Monday morning, I'll tell Dad."

"And Guy?"

"Sunday night." Which meant that for my meeting with Dad on Monday morning, I'd probably have a black eye. "Once Guy comes back from that party he's going to in Big Sky."

"Okay." Her frame deflated. "Thank you. I know he's going to be as mad as a hater but . . . he'll get over it."

"You're welcome." A smile tugged at the corner of my mouth. This woman and her messed-up sayings. "And it's as mad as a hatter."

"I know. But—"

"You like your version better."

"Yeah. Haters gonna hate."

"You got that one right."

She gave me a small smile. "I guess so."

"I don't like this either, Stell. The secrets. I swear." But we had years, right? What was a few days of hiding when we had years and years to share this with the world? "Tomorrow. Want to try this again? Just you and me?"

And hopefully, date attempt number three wouldn't be a disaster.

"Actually . . . my best friend Wendy invited me out. She works at a gym in town and they're having a party at The Crystal."

"Oh, okay." Damn. I'd hoped to be with her on New Year's Eve.

"Want to come along? As my date?"

The invitation felt a lot like a test.

I wasn't one for failing tests.

"Yes."

She must have thought I'd say no because the smile she sent me was full of relief. "Are you going to come inside?"

"If you'll let me."

She stepped aside and crooked a finger.

CHAPTER ELEVEN

STELLA

Wendy's eyes bugged out as Heath and I walked into The Crystal Bar. From across the crowded room, her jaw dropped when she saw his hand on my shoulder. In a blink, the shock disappeared and she sent me a scowl.

I had explaining to do.

"Sorry," I mouthed.

"You're in trouble," she mouthed back.

I reached for Heath's hand, clasping it tight, as I weaved through the crush.

The bar was packed for New Year's Eve. Women were dressed in shimmering tops and shiny dresses. A cluster of men had noisemakers, blowing them after a round of shots. We were hours from midnight and that sound would get old soon. Party hats and tiaras with the upcoming year's number were scattered on the bar. Foil curlicues hung from the bar's dusty rafters.

The Crystal Bar, though fancy in name, was the roughest bar on Main. It was the definition of no frills. It had yet to be renovated and changed to an upscale, trendy bar like so many others downtown.

Rows of old keg taps were hung high on one of the bar's brick walls, joining the beer and liquor signs. One section of the ceiling had been dedicated to confiscated fake IDs, row after row of them covered safe behind a sheet of Plexiglas. The Crystal had a smell of its own, cultivated from too many years of old drunks and rowdy college kids. The number one Yelp review ridiculed the dive bar for the lewd signs, foul language and filthy bathrooms.

"This place reminds me of college," Heath said, leaning close so I could hear him over the noise.

"Me too." I laughed. "Same musty smell. Same cobwebs."

He chuckled. "Pretty much."

We were older than most of the people here tonight by at least five years. But considering Wendy worked with a lot of college students at the gym, it was no surprise they'd chosen this as their party spot.

"What do you want to drink?" Heath asked. "I'll go order. You can talk to Wendy."

"Champagne if they have any."

"Okay, baby." He bent and brushed a kiss to my cheek

and the thrill of his lips on my skin raced through my veins.

We were here. In public. No hiding. No pretending.

No secrets.

I practically danced my way to Wendy. She was frowning, but I couldn't help my smile. "Happy New Year."

"All done crushing on Heath Holiday, huh?"

"Not quite." I blushed, finding him at the bar. He stood taller than the other men, his shoulders broader. As he waited for the bartender, he pushed the sleeves of his black sweater up his sinewed forearms.

"Spill. Right now." Wendy smacked me on the shoulder. "How long has this been going on? And why wasn't I the first person you called?"

"Sorry. It started at the party on Christmas Eve. But we haven't told Guy yet, or my boss. So we've been keeping it quiet."

"You didn't trust me to keep a secret? Like I'd ever talk to Guy. Or your boss."

"I know." I sighed. "Forgive me?"

"Only if you tell me everything."

I smiled. "I'm having sex with Heath Holiday."

She giggled. "Someone should. Look at that man. He's gorgeous."

I glanced over my shoulder, laughing with her. "I still can't believe it. I just want to scream it, like that will help make it real."

"Do it." She nudged my elbow. "It's so loud in here no one will even hear you."

Neil Diamond's "Sweet Caroline" was blaring over the speakers, most of the crowd joining in at the *Da. Da. Da.* line. The men with the noisemakers were going berserk, honking and blowing their horns.

If there was ever a place to scream, this was it.

Screw it. "I'm having sex with Heath Holiday!"

Halfway through my sentence, the music cut out. The noisemakers stopped. All eyes swung my way and Wendy cringed on my behalf.

"Oh my God," I whispered, shrinking into myself.

"Uh . . ." The bartender had stopped the music to grab the microphone. "Good for you, lady. And Heath Holiday."

I dropped my face to my hands as the room laughed. Why? Why me?

"Anyway," the bartender drawled. "Quick announcement. Draft pints from now until power hour at eleven are two bucks."

The music started again as abruptly as it had stopped.

I didn't move other than to let my hair drape around me, shielding my face. Tonight, I was wearing a cream sweater and a pair of silver, sequined pants. It was my disco-ball outfit. What I wouldn't give to be in all-black so I could slink into a shadow and disappear.

A strong arm banded around my shoulders, pulling me

into a rock-solid chest. A chest I'd slept on every night this week.

"This is my fault, isn't it?" Heath bent low to speak in my ear.

"Yes. All of my embarrassing moments are your fault, remember? You're cursed."

"Sorry."

I relaxed and dropped my hands, spinning to face him. "How bad was it?"

Heath set his beer bottle and my champagne on the table closest to us, then he framed my face with his hands before tipping his head up and shouting, "I'm having sex with Stella Marten!"

The room was too loud, and the only people who heard him were close by.

"See?" he asked. "Not that bad."

"Ugh." I groaned and fell forward into his body. "That is not the same."

He wrapped me up tight, kissing my hair. "Hi. I'm Heath."

"Wendy."

I stayed buried in his chest as he shook her hand.

"What are your intentions with my best friend?"

I groaned again. "Wendy."

"That's a good fucking question."

Except Wendy hadn't asked it.

I stiffened at the angry, familiar voice. So did Heath. It came from over his shoulder.

As Heath's arms loosened, I peeled myself away, peering past him to see my brother.

Maybe the entire bar hadn't heard Heath's announcement. But Guy had. He stood fuming, as livid as I'd seen him in years. My brother wore his emotions on his face, and at the moment, he was close to a rage.

Only one time in my life had I seen Guy this angry.

And that had landed an epic asshole in the hospital.

"Oh, shit," Wendy muttered, coming to my side. "He's pissed."

"You think?" I deadpanned, then shifted, trying to squeeze in between Heath and Guy.

But Heath felt me move and cut me off. One of his hands clasped mine as he spoke to Guy. "Let me explain."

"Fuck you," Guy said. "Fuck your explanation."

"Guy," I hissed.

"Don't." He pointed at my nose. "You kept this from me too."

"We were going to tell you," Heath said. "When you got back from skiing at Big Sky."

"Surprise. Mel showed up and one of us had to leave. So I came home early, thinking I'd call my best friend and my sister. See if they wanted to meet up. Then neither of them answered so I came downtown. And here you are."

"I'm sorry," I said.

Guy had already dismissed me, his gaze locked with Heath's.

"Take it easy," Heath said. "Let us explain."

"Calm down, Guy." I reached for his arm but he jerked away, sparing me a brief sneer before narrowing his eyes on Heath.

"After everything I told you the other night." Guy scoffed. "I can't fucking believe you."

"What?" I looked up to Heath. "What did he tell you?"

"This is not the same." Heath's jaw clenched. "Don't you dare compare me to that motherfucker."

Wait. What had Guy told him? There could only be one story. A story that Guy had no right to share, especially with Heath.

No. My head started spinning and I clutched Heath's hand for balance. This wasn't happening. There was a reason I didn't tell people about what happened to me freshman year. It just wasn't an embarrassing story. It had been a nightmare.

Guy had no right.

"You told him." I stepped closer to my brother. "You told him about Dave."

Guy didn't even have the decency to look guilty. "Yeah, I told him. I knew you were seeing someone. Sneaking around. I was worried about you and asked Heath if he knew who you were seeing. And he lied to me. You lied. To. My. Face. Some friend."

Most of those words were swallowed up by the noise in my head.

Heath knew about Dave. He'd known that one of

Guy's friends had drugged me and would have raped me. He'd known all week.

He'd known the night he'd come over and asked if I could keep a secret.

My stomach dropped.

"How could you?" Guy asked him. "She's my sister. You were supposed to be my best friend. What happens when you fuck her over? What happens when you break her heart?"

"That's not—"

"Gonna happen?" Guy arched his eyebrows. "Sure it is."

"Stop." My voice was too soft. Neither of them heard me, and Guy was on a roll.

"You're using her. I told you she's had a crush on you and you decided she'd be easy prey, right? An easy lay?"

"Watch your goddamn mouth." Heath inched closer to Guy. "You will not talk about Stella like she's some cheap score."

"You're treating her like one."

"That's not what this is. I care about her. I would never intentionally hurt her."

"Stop." I managed to make my voice a little louder. But it didn't do any good. It was still too loud.

Guy scoffed, still ignoring me. "You've said that about all your women. You never intentionally hurt anyone, but you do. Over and over. I've watched them cry over you when you've moved on."

"And you're so much better?"

"Fuck you," Guy spat. "This isn't about me. It's about you and my sister."

"Stop." I tore my hand from Heath's. "Stop talking about me like I'm not standing here."

"I hate you for this." Guy's jaw ticked and he turned like he was going to leave, but before he took a step, he spun, moving so fast I barely had time to register what was coming.

Heath saw it. He didn't even try to move. He just let Guy's knuckles collide with his jaw.

The smack echoed around us.

Wendy cried out, gripping my arm to pull me away.

But Heath put his hand on my arm, keeping me behind him as he grunted.

The bouncers rushed toward our corner of the bar, shouting and shoving people out of the way.

I held my breath, staring between Guy and Heath, unblinking. *Don't fight. Please, don't fight.*

Heath stood tall, glowering at Guy.

And my brother glowered back.

But thankfully, no more punches were thrown.

"You're both out." One of the bouncers took Guy's elbow, attempting to drag him away. Except the bouncers were all smaller than Guy and Heath.

"Let me go." Guy tore his arm free, and this time when he turned, he didn't stop until he was out the front door. A bouncer followed him outside.

"You have to leave," another bouncer told Heath.

"I'm going." Heath held up his hands as the bouncer shoved at his shoulder, pushing him toward the rear exit.

"Oh my God." Wendy's hand found mine.

I gripped it tight, staring at Heath's tall body as he waded past clusters of people. Most of them were oblivious to what had just happened. Even those in Wendy's party hadn't been paying much attention.

"Come on." I hauled Wendy with me as I pushed through the room.

Guy was furious. The only person who'd be able to talk to him right now was me. But I didn't walk toward the front. I chose the back door.

I chose Heath.

He stood in the snow-covered parking lot across the alley. His hand was on his jaw, rubbing the spot where he'd been hit. When he heard me coming, his hand fell away and he strode toward us.

"Are you okay?" he asked.

"Yes." I gulped. "Are you?"

"I'm fine," he grumbled. "I was expecting it."

He seemed so . . . calm. Meanwhile, my heart was galloping in my chest. My breath came in heavy pants, the cold air turning it into a billowing cloud around us.

"I'm going back in to get my coat." Wendy pried her hand from mine. "Wait for me."

"Okay." I nodded, taking a minute to breathe as she rushed toward the bar. "That was . . ."

"I'm sorry." He dragged a hand through his hair. "Christ."

"The night you went to his house, what did he tell you?"

Heath's eyes darted to mine. "Stell, it doesn't matter."

"What did he tell you?" I gritted my teeth.

He blew out a long breath. "He told me about his friend. The buddy from school. Dave. That he took you out to a frat party. That you guys kept it a secret. And that it, um . . . ended badly."

"He drugged me. He would have raped me."

Heath flinched. "Don't say that."

"Why not? It's true. It's the most humiliating moment of my life. The one *not* your fault."

My joke fell flat.

Heath looked like he was in more pain now than he had been after Guy'd slammed a fist into his face.

"I didn't want you to know," I admitted. "Guy had no right to tell you that story. Is that why you wanted us to be a secret?"

"What?"

"Is this a pity thing?" I asked. "Is that why?"

"You weren't a secret in that bar, Stella." He pointed over my shoulder, the tension rising on his face. "I told you I was going to tell Guy. This has nothing to do with what that fucker did to you in college."

So why couldn't I get this icky feeling out of my stomach?

"This is not how I expected it to be tonight," I whispered and my chin began to quiver.

Heath reached for me, but I stepped out of his grasp. If he touched me, I'd melt. If he held me, I'd cry.

"I have to talk to Guy."

"We can go see him tomorrow. Together."

I shook my head. "No. Now."

"Okay." He took another step but I held up a hand.

"Alone. He's my brother."

When I'd fallen off a swing set or monkey bars, Guy had always been the first to rush to my side. If I'd crashed my bike, he'd been the one to hold my hand while Dad had picked the gravel from my skinned knees. Guy had watched out for me in high school, scaring the creeps away with his threats. He'd tried to do the same in college too.

I suspected that most of Guy's anger and frustration were not because of Heath. But because of me. Because I'd kept a secret. I'd let Heath convince me that he needed to be the one to tell Guy. But that had been a mistake.

I should have told him.

Guy should have heard it from me.

"Stell—"

"Tell Wendy I'll call her." I jogged away, rushing as fast as I could without risking a fall on the snow in my heeled boots.

"Stella!" Heath called, but I didn't slow.

I reached the end of the alley, rounded the corner and

raced to the sidewalk on Main, scanning both directions for Guy.

He hadn't gone far. Just outside The Crystal Bar, my brother paced, his hands balled in fists. Maybe he'd expected us to come out the front door too.

"Guy," I hollered, rushing to his side.

He stopped pacing and looked over my shoulder like he was expecting Heath.

"I'm alone," I said, slowing to a stop.

The adrenaline was ebbing and the chill seeped through my sweater. These pants were cute but not exactly warm. I wrapped my arms around my waist. "I'm sorry."

"You don't know what you're doing, Stella."

"I'm not a kid anymore, Guy. I know what I'm doing."

"He's not who you think he is."

"Guy." I gave him a sad smile. "This is Heath. I know exactly who he is. He's kind. He's gracious. He's smart. He whistles while he shaves and loves his family. He's loyal, so much so that he asked me to keep this a secret because he knew you were going to freak out."

"A secret? He asked you to be a secret? That's suspect, Stell. Not sweet."

"I care about him. I have since I was a little girl."

"Exactly." He threw up his arms. "You've built him into this dream or fantasy. What happens when the illusion falls to shit? What happens when you realize he's a womanizer? That he's using you and you'll be tossed aside when he's done?"

"That's not going to happen." I believed that down to the marrow of my bones. Heath wasn't using me. This was real.

We were real.

"Yes, it is!" Guy dragged a hand through his hair. "He's a player. I know because we're not that different. You know why Mel dumped me? Because I was hitting on another woman. It was stupid. It was a dumb-fuck move. But I was drinking and this girl wanted to flirt. Mel showed and caught me about two seconds from kissing another woman. She broke it off and told me never to call her again."

My heart twisted for my idiot brother. "I'm sorry."

"It's my fault."

"Yeah, it is. But that doesn't mean Heath will do the same to me."

"I've seen him play women, Stell."

"When? In high school? College? You know Heath. You know him. Do you actually think he'd play me?"

A flicker of doubt crossed his gaze, but he didn't give in. He just raised that stubborn chin.

"Whatever." I tossed up my hands. There was no talking to him tonight. He'd made up his mind, and nothing I could say would change it. "If he plays me, then I'll dump him as Mel dumped you."

"And I'll lose my best friend."

"I'm not asking you to choose."

He blinked. "Seriously? Like I could be friends with a man who hurt my sister."

If only my brother could be as loyal to his girlfriends as he was to me. "I don't know what will happen with Heath. But you can't protect me all the time."

"Break up with him, Stella. End this now before it goes too far."

I huffed. "No."

"Yes."

"This isn't your business, Guy. You don't get to tell me what to do."

"Then don't come crying to me when he breaks your heart. I won't be there to dry your tears. Not this time." With that, he turned and marched down the sidewalk, leaving me standing alone.

My chin was quivering again, not just from the cold.

I was seconds away from crying when a pair of strong, familiar arms and a comforting scent wrapped around me.

Heath hadn't left. Of course, he hadn't left. He'd never leave me like this. Something Guy would know if he pulled his head out of his ass.

Heath had probably hovered around the corner, out of sight, but listening to our entire conversation.

"Come on, baby." Heath held me tighter. "Let's go home."

CHAPTER TWELVE

STELLA

"So much for a fun New Year's Eve, huh?" I dropped my gaze to my lap as Heath drove us across town toward his place.

When I'd been getting ready earlier tonight, taking care with my hair and makeup, I'd been off-the-charts giddy to end one year and kick off another with Heath by my side. Now all I wanted to do was wash the glittery eye shadow from my lids and strip out of these sequined pants.

This disco ball had deflated.

Our entire week of dates had been a disaster. Was that a sign that this relationship was a mistake? Were we doomed?

"Hey." Heath reached across the console and brushed his thumb over my cheek. "Don't give up on the night yet. We've still got an hour until midnight."

I gave him a sad smile. "Maybe you should just take me home. Then we can start fresh tomorrow."

"No. You can start fresh from my place." He nodded to the backseat. "Besides, you already packed."

Actually, he'd packed. My suitcase was on the floor behind us. I'd had everything stuffed in a backpack when he'd arrived to pick me up tonight. Like the other night, the bag had been stuffed until the seams had strained. Heath had taken one look at it, then marched to my closet to drag out a suitcase.

"Okay." I checked my phone for the hundredth time since we'd climbed in the truck.

Still nothing from Guy.

When we'd returned to the alley, Wendy had been waiting. She'd opted to stay downtown, understanding why I hadn't been in the mood for a party. She probably would have come home with me but Heath hadn't given her the chance to offer. After my argument with Guy, he'd spared me only a moment to hug Wendy before putting me in his truck and cranking on the heat.

In the distance, a golden firework exploded in the sky. Its tendrils faded to nothing as my eyes filled with tears.

"It hurts that he doesn't want me to be happy," I whispered.

"I'm sorry, baby. This is my fault."

"No, it's his." A tear fell. "How can he not want me to have you?"

"Don't cry." His hand came to my shoulder, sliding to my neck. "Or wait until we get home so I can hold you."

I sniffled but the battle was lost. The tears came in a steady stream, and by the time we eased into his garage, I was sure that my glitter shadow and mascara were all over my face.

Heath shut off the truck and climbed out, rounding the hood to open my door.

As he scooped me out, I buried my face in the crook of his neck and let him carry me inside. "Guy sucks."

He chuckled. "Tonight? Yes."

"How's your face?" I lifted up to look at the red spot on his jaw.

"It'll be fine. Not the first time I've been punched."

"Really? Who else has hit you?" And how did I not know about this?

"Tobias and Maddox when we were kids." He shrugged. "Brothers fight."

"Oh." I dropped my head to his shoulder again. "Guy and I don't really fight."

"He'll deal. When he sees that we're serious, he'll come around."

"You're right. But in the meantime, I'm going to give him the silent treatment. The jerk. I mean . . . you're his best friend. How could he even say that stuff about you? Doesn't that piss you off? That he would think you're bad for me? Because it pisses me off."

A surge of anger streaked through my veins. Anger

was good. It dried up the tears, and as Heath set me on the end of his bed, I harrumphed and crossed my arms over my chest. "He doesn't get to talk about you like that."

"Defending my honor?" Heath slid off one of my shoes.

"Yes."

"It's sexy as hell." His fingers skimmed my ankle before he moved to the other shoe, taking it off and tossing it aside. Then his hands trailed up my legs, moving for the waistband of my pants.

If anger had beaten out the sadness, lust was going to kick anger's ass.

I lifted a hand to Heath's hair, messing up the strands that he'd combed earlier. "Will you kiss me at midnight?"

"Stupid question, Stell."

I fisted his hair, giving it a yank. "Are you teasing me?"

"Always." He chuckled and shifted closer, walking on his knees before brushing his lips to mine. "All of your midnight kisses are mine. New Year's Eve or not. You're mine."

Mine. That was a word I'd listen to on repeat as long as it came from his deep voice.

I leaned in, wanting another kiss, but he backed away and a look of concern marred his handsome features. "What?"

"About the thing in college. When Guy told me, it shocked the hell out of me. I wasn't sure what to say. I should have brought it up this week, but . . . every time I think about it, I get mad. I'm so sorry that happened to you."

"It's okay." I took his hand off my knee, lacing our fingers together. "It could have been a lot worse, and it's behind me."

"Should we talk about it?"

"I've talked about it. Guy thinks it's a secret, but Mom knows. She encouraged me to go to therapy. It's embarrassing that I put myself in that position. That I trusted someone who I shouldn't have. Those emotions will probably always be there. I learned a hard lesson. But otherwise, it's in the past."

"If you ever want to talk, I'm here."

"Thank you." I leaned in for a kiss, but he denied me again.

He grinned as I frowned. "You'll get what you're after soon enough."

"What are you waiting for?"

"I'm sorry I asked you to be a secret." He cupped my face with his hands. "No more secrets."

Something unlocked in my chest. The feeling of doubt that he really wanted me. I didn't know how much I needed to hear that until the words were out of his mouth.

"You're beautiful," he said. "You're smart. You're hilarious, and your quirks are enchanting."

"I don't have quirks."

"Disagree to agree." He smiled. "I respect you, Stella. I can't say that I've always treated women the right way. I'm not proud of it. I don't know where this thing will go, but I'll always respect you."

"I know you will."

"No more secrets."

I shook my head. "No more secrets."

"I'll talk to Dad on Monday. I'm guessing he won't care but will ask that we don't broadcast it in the office."

"Fine by me." I needed time at Holiday Homes to establish myself. I didn't need my peers or clients thinking I was getting preferential treatment because I was dating Heath.

"Good." This time when I leaned in, he met me in the middle for the kiss I wanted.

The kiss that erased the tension from the night. The kiss that assured me there'd be no more hiding. The kiss that promised it would be okay.

That one kiss led to another and another until we were connected in every way. Breathless, skin against skin, it was at midnight with Heath buried inside of me that I stopped crushing on Heath Holiday.

And fell in love with him instead.

―――――

"YOU KNOW what I don't know about you?" Heath asked as we stood in the kitchen the next morning.

"What?"

"How do you like your coffee? I should know. I've seen

you get some at work. But I was too busy staring at your ass to remember if you added cream or sugar."

"Cream and sugar."

"Sweet." He pulled me into his chest. "Like you. I should have guessed."

The coffee pot brewed on the counter beside us.

We'd slept in this morning because he'd kept me up late. I'd woken in his arms and after he'd made love to me again, we'd hopped in the shower before dressing in sweats. Heath had asked me to spend the day here. Just the two of us.

As the start of a new year went, this one was the best I'd ever had.

"What should we have for break—"

The doorbell rang, cutting him off.

He grumbled. "So much for our day alone."

"What if we just ignored it?"

"Good plan." We stood motionless, our gazes aimed in the direction of the door.

The doorbell rang again, not just once, but five times.

"There's only one person who does that." *Guy.* I looked up to Heath's jaw. There was a faint bruise forming but the stubble disguised most of it. "We can ignore him."

"Your call, baby."

My nostrils flared. "I don't want him to wreck our day. But I want to hear what he has to say."

"All right."

"We'll give him five minutes. Either he apologizes in those minutes or we boot him into the snow."

"I'll do the booting."

I laughed. "Piece of chocolate cake."

Heath opened his mouth but instead of correcting me, he simply smiled. "I love chocolate cake."

"Me too. Let's make one later."

"As long as you do the baking."

"You got it."

He let me go and took my hand, walking us to the door. He opened it, but stepped aside so I could take the lead.

Guy stood on the porch.

With Wendy.

"Hi." I smiled at her, then glared at my brother. "What?"

"Can we come inside?" he asked. "It's cold out here."

"Then you should have brought a coat."

"Stella."

I waved Wendy inside. "She can come in. You can't."

"Morning." Wendy pulled her lips together to hide a smile as she crossed the threshold. "Happy New Year."

"Happy New Year." I glanced between her and Guy. She had a green smoothie in her hand. Guy had another. Unlike me, he'd drank half the cup. "How did you two wind up together?"

"After you guys left last night, our party moved to another bar," she said. "I found this idiot there, drunk.

And because I'm a better person than he is, I let him sleep it off on my couch."

"Ah." I nodded.

"Stella." Guy's teeth were chattering. "Please."

"No. You're a jerkface, butthole loser."

As kids, that had been the ultimate insult. I had no idea why it had popped into my head, but it did and well . . . it fit.

Heath's chest shook with silent laughter.

Wendy snorted.

"I know," Guy muttered.

"You hurt my feelings. Asshole." *So there.* A grown woman's insult.

"I'm sorry," he said.

"Good." *Victory.* "Now you may come inside. But mostly because I'm cold too, and you're letting all of the heat out."

Guy stepped inside and kicked the snow from his boots. He'd been pretty focused on me, but he risked a glance at Heath. "How's the jaw?"

Heath shrugged. "Stella kissed it better."

Wendy, who'd been sipping her smoothie, choked on her drink, coughing and sputtering. "Oh, God, I love this. I'm so glad neither of you are taking it easy on him."

"I regret getting in your car last night," Guy told her.

"Keep groveling, Marten," Wendy ordered. "Get back on your figurative knees so we can leave these two alone to enjoy their day."

He sighed but didn't argue. Then he squared his shoulders and faced Heath. "I love my sister."

"I know."

"I don't want her to get hurt."

"I'm not going to hurt her." There was such conviction in Heath's voice.

Guy heard it. So did Wendy.

She leaned against my arm and swooned.

"Good." Guy nodded, then faced me. "Heath's my best friend."

"I know."

"I don't want him to get hurt either."

I nodded, my heart swelling. For such a pain in my ass, he really had a soft heart.

"I'm sorry about what I said last night." Guy stepped closer, holding his arms out. "Forgive me?"

"Yes." I stepped into his hug. But one sniff and I shoved him away. "You stink like the bar."

"Wendy wouldn't let me shower." His stomach growled. "And all she'd give me for breakfast was this disgusting green goo."

"It's healthy," she and I said in unison.

Heath stepped up and clapped Guy on the shoulder. "We were about to make breakfast. Want to stick around?"

Guy nodded. "As long as Stella's cooking and not you."

"I'm cooking," I said.

"Mind if I hop in the shower?" Guy asked, sniffing his own armpit and grimacing.

"Go for it." Heath jerked his head down the hallway toward the guest bathroom. "I'll grab you some clothes."

As Guy disappeared, Wendy sighed. "My work here is done."

"Thank you for taking him home." I hugged her. "And bringing him here."

"You're welcome."

"What are you doing today?"

"Nothing much. Why?"

"Want to stick around?"

She looked between the two of us. "You don't mind?"

"Stay," Heath told her.

I smiled and skipped to the kitchen to make us all breakfast. After our plates were clear and the dishwasher was running, we moved to the living room.

"Should we watch something?" Heath asked.

"I wish the last season of *State of Ruin* was out on Madcast," I told Heath as we snuggled on the couch.

"Maddox gave me early access."

I gasped and sat up straight. "And you're just telling me this now?"

"We've had a busy week. There was no time for TV."

"True." I settled into his arms as he pulled up the wildly popular show and hit play. "It feels longer than a week."

He held me tighter. "Because it was always supposed to be you and me, Stell."

"Would you two shut the fuck up?" Guy barked from the recliner. "I want to watch."

Heath responded by swiping up a toss pillow and throwing it at my brother's face.

"I need to go home," Guy said, swatting the pillow away, but he made no move to leave.

"I never did get into this show." Wendy was curled into the end of a loveseat, her eyes closed as she burrowed beneath a throw blanket. "I'm taking a nap."

"Shh," Guy hissed.

Heath laughed and stretched out behind me, curling an arm around me as I fit my back to his chest as the opening credits played. "Happy New Year."

"Happy New Year."

He leaned in to whisper in my ear. "Do you believe it yet?"

I met his bright eyes. I saw the promise in his gaze. We'd only been together for a week. But this was the week that everything had changed.

Heath Holiday was mine.

"I believe it."

EPILOGUE
HEATH

One year later ...

"Was it this loud last year?" Stella asked as we swayed on the dance floor at my parents' annual Christmas party.

"Yes, but we missed the loud parts."

"Right." She gave me a dreamy smile. "Because you were sucking my nipples in the sitting room."

The couple dancing next to us gave her a sideways look, but Stella was too busy surveying the ballroom to notice.

I pressed a kiss to her temple and spun her in the other direction. She blamed me for her embarrassing moments, and over the past year, I'd taken the fall many times to keep the smile on her face. But the real culprit behind this curse was Stella's verbal filter—or lack thereof.

"These guys are the best." Stella nodded toward the

stage. "Good choice."

"Thanks, baby."

The live band was rocking The Baxter. Maybe I was biased because Mom had put me in charge of music this year, but I saw more people dancing than in years past.

For the first time, my parents had relinquished some control over this annual Holiday event and had enlisted their sons to help.

I'd been in charge of music. Tobias had been assigned decorations. And Maddox had volunteered for food and drinks. His daughter's sweet tooth would not go unsatisfied tonight because the dessert table was twice as long as usual.

"Oh, no," Stella groaned.

"What?"

"Joe Jensen is coming this way." She put on a fake smile, pretending to be glad to see him. "Hey, Joe."

"Hi, Stella." He stopped close enough that it forced us to stop dancing. "Say . . . I was thinking about the kitchen earlier and before I forget, I'd like to change the design."

She tensed but that smile never faltered. "Okay. What are you thinking?"

"Can we make room for a subzero fridge and a professional-grade range?"

Joe had just told her last week that he didn't cook much. But my beautiful wife didn't throw that in his face. She simply nodded. "You got it. I'll work up the numbers for you next week."

"You're the best. Heath, she deserves a raise."

"Noted." I chuckled, waiting for him to disappear into the crowd before I swept her into my arms again. "You're going to win the bet, aren't you?"

"Easily."

"Damn."

This summer, we'd made a bet about Joe Jensen's house and when it would be finished. I'd figured it would be done by New Year's. She'd promised it would take well into spring. Given his constant change orders and the specialty products he wanted in each room, it was now the longest-running project in Holiday Homes history.

And through it all, Stella had managed it perfectly. Not only had she won Joe over, but she'd won our bet and got to pick our next vacation spot.

"I'm thinking Hawaii," she said.

"Last time you said Alaska."

"I changed my mind. I don't think I'll be up for hiking this summer."

"Why not?"

She took a deep breath, then dropped a hand to splay across her belly.

"Wha—" Holy. Shit. "Does that mean what I think it means?"

"Yeah." The light in her eyes danced.

A rush of fear and anxiety and excitement hit me all at once and I had to stop moving before I tripped over my own damn feet. Was this happening?

"You're pregnant?"

She giggled. "I'm pregnant."

My arms snaked around her and I crushed her to my chest. "I love you. Fuck, but I love you."

"I love you too." She clung to me as I buried my face in her hair, drawing in that smell and letting it steady me.

My beautiful, amazing wife was having our baby.

"When did you find out?"

"Right before we left the house."

"That's why you were in the bathroom so long."

She nodded. "I would have told you then, but I wanted to be alone."

This, us on the crowded dance floor, was as alone as we'd been all night.

Guy and Wendy had been at home with us earlier, the women getting ready together. Then we'd all ridden to the hotel in my truck. Stella had been quiet on the drive, but I'd thought it was just because Guy and Wendy had been arguing.

Or . . . *debating*. They called their arguments debates.

Never in a million years would I have put those two together as a couple. They *debated* all the time, rarely agreeing on anything. But Guy was nuts over her and the way Wendy looked at him, well . . . it was the way I'd catch Stella looking at me.

"Are you happy?" she asked.

I nodded, holding her closer. "So happy."

Next to our wedding day, this was the happiest day of my life.

We'd only been married for a few months, but nothing with Stella had ever felt rushed. She'd always been a part of my life. She'd been that missing piece. When her lease ran out on her apartment this summer, she'd moved in. Two weeks later, I'd proposed. We'd planned a fall wedding and the day she'd walked down the aisle wearing a white lace dress and my diamond on her finger was the day she'd made my whole life.

"You're going to be the best mom."

"Stop." She pinched my ribs. "You're going to make me cry."

I leaned away, framing her face in my hands. Then I kissed her like we were home in our bedroom, not surrounded by family and friends. When I broke away, she had a pretty flush to her cheeks. "This is why you didn't want champagne."

"Yeah."

"Hey, Heath. Hi, Stella." Gretchen danced over with her husband. "How are you guys tonight?"

"Good." I clutched Stella's hand. "Having fun?"

"It's always a fun night."

"We're going to grab some dessert," I lied, taking Stella's hand in mine and leading her off the floor.

There'd be time to tell friends later. There'd be lots of celebrating. But what I really wanted was a minute alone with my woman. We weaved through the crush, nodding and smiling as people said hello. Then we escaped the ballroom and I pulled her to the same place where we'd started a year ago.

The sitting room was empty. It looked the same as it had last year. The second the door swung closed, I had Stella in my arms again, my mouth sealed over hers.

She gave a little laugh, a breath hitch, then kissed me back. When she wrapped one leg around my hip, I pressed my arousal into her center. My hand cupped her breast and my fingers were tugging at the fabric of her dress when the door flew open.

"Oh, hell," Guy muttered. "Get a room."

Stella and I broke apart to see him and Wendy both averting their eyes.

"We did." I dried my lips and made sure Stella's dress was covering her nipple.

"Get a room with a locking door," he said, dragging Wendy out and leaving us alone.

Stella giggled. "We should probably go back."

"Yeah. But we're leaving early."

"We can't. Remember we promised your mom we'd help clean up."

I frowned. "I'll get us out of it."

"No, don't. We'll help. It might even be fun."

I raised an eyebrow. "It will not be fun."

"Cleaning can be fun."

"Baby, I love you, but no. We're not staying."

She smiled. "Disagree to agree."

THE NAUGHTY, THE NICE AND THE NANNY

One week with one little girl—an angel, according to my staffing agency. Acting as the short-term nanny for a single dad should have been an easy way to make some extra cash. Until I show up for my first day and face off with a demon disguised as a seven-year-old girl wearing a red tutu and matching glitter slippers.

Oh, and her father? My temporary boss? Maddox Holiday. The same Maddox Holiday I crushed on in high school. The same Maddox Holiday who didn't even know I existed. And the same Maddox Holiday who hasn't set foot in Montana for years because he's been too busy running his billionaire empire.

Enduring seven days is going to feel like scaling the Himalayas in six-inch heels. Toss in the Holiday family's annual soiree, and Christmas Eve nightmares really do come true. But I can do anything for a week, especially for this paycheck, even if it means wrangling the naughty, impressing the nice, and playing the nanny.

A PARTRIDGE AND A PREGNANCY

There are a lot of places I'd rather spend Christmas Eve morning than on a cold, snowy sidewalk outside someone else's home. I'd kill to be sitting beside a fireplace, drinking cocoa, wearing flannel pajamas and reading a book.

Instead, I'm here, standing in front of my one-night stand's house, working up the courage to ring the doorbell and tell him I'm pregnant.

I hate that term—one-night stand. It sounds so cheap and sleezy. Tobias Holiday is neither of those things. He's handsome and caring. Witty and charismatic. And once, a long time ago, he was mine.

Our one-night reunion was only supposed to be a hookup. A fling with an old lover. A parting farewell before I moved to London and put my feelings for him an ocean away. How exactly am I supposed to explain that to

Tobias that I'm having a baby? His baby? Maybe I could sing it. He always loved the silly songs I made up in the shower.

Three French hens, two turtle doves.

And a partridge and a pregnancy.

ACKNOWLEDGMENTS

Happy Holidays! I hope this book was as fun for you to read as it was for me to write. On a whim, I decided last Christmas to write three stories for this Christmas. I dragged it out over the course of months because that Christmas cheer was such a joy to add to my every day.

A huge thanks to my editing and proofreading team: Marion, Karen, Judy and Julie. Thank you to Sarah Hansen for the cutest covers in the world. Thanks to my agent, Kimberly, and the team at Brower Literary. And my publicist, Nina, and the team at Valentine PR.

Thanks to the members of Perry and Nash. I'm not sure how I got so lucky to have such an incredible reader group for both my Devney Perry and my Willa Nash books, but know that your love and support mean the world to me.

The same is true for the amazing bloggers who read and promote my stories. I am so grateful for you all!

And lastly, thanks to Bill, Will and Nash. I wrote these books in the evenings and love that you let me take an hour here and there to play with these characters.

ABOUT THE AUTHOR

Willa Nash is *USA Today* Bestselling Author Devney Perry's alter ego, writing contemporary romance stories for Kindle Unlimited. Lover of Swedish Fish, hater of laundry, she lives in Washington State with her husband and two sons. She was born and raised in Montana and has a passion for writing books in the state she calls home.

Don't miss out on Willa's latest book news.
Subscribe to her newsletter!
www.willanash.com

Made in the USA
Coppell, TX
01 December 2022

87542639R00121